Full Circle

Dying in Plain Sight

Full Circle

Dying in Plain Sight

Robbin Washington

COPYRIGHT

ISBN-13: 978-1-947656-54-3

ISBN10: 1947656546

The Butterfly Typeface Publishing
PO BOX 56193
Little Rock Arkansas 72215
www.butterflytypeface.com
butterflytypeface.imw@gmail.com

DEDICATION

With total love and admiration, I dedicate FULL CIRCLE to some very special people that I've known all my life, and that know me well.

First and foremost, my husband Winston, you are the one that loved me through the pain and kept me grounded, you will ALWAYS be my very best friend. My children, all six of them give me a reason to keep loving and writing. My very close friend Ellis, without you, this book may have landed in the wrong hands, and also to your wife Renee, who knew something was wrong, even if you couldn't quite put your finger on it. Ebony, Tiffany, Tonya, and LaChaun, you four were there when my life took a major dip, thank you for being my REAL FRIENDS.

And last but certainly not least, my Mom. You always read every word before anyone else, I know you are still my biggest cheerleader in heaven, and God, you guided my hands and my heart.

"I'm thankful for all my scars, because they only make my heart...GRATEFUL!"

-Rita Ora

TABLE OF CONTENTS

FOREWORD

In describing my relationship with Robbin Washington, I simply describe it as 'having the best of both worlds.' She is a mother/sister figure with a splash of friendship and fun. She's my Aunt as well as my friend. God ordained her title, but we secured our bond; a bond created by the sharing of the same pain that all too often goes unseen and unspoken.

"Full Circle" allows the reader to walk in the boots of a woman beaten by life, battered by love and bruised by one's own judgment. You will experience every low and every high, every storm and the rainbow that follows. You'll be encouraged and inspired by this author's story of love, heartache, and survival.

In a world where domestic violence all too often goes unnoticed but not unseen, unspoken of - but often discussed, you'll see that every fight doesn't have to be a physical one to find the fighter you have within.

There once was a time when I too was beaten by life, battered by love and bruised by my own judgment. A survivor myself, I was able to empathize with the pain Robbin Washington shares, as well as celebrate the joys she describes.

Robbin Washington captured my heart as a human being and channeled my inner strength as a woman. With every page read you too will find a connection to this author as you embrace her work.

Carla Washington

ACKNOWLEDGMENTS

I would like to acknowledge the following people for staying on me to FINISH IT:

First and Foremost, my Mother Marie

My Husband and True Best Friend, Winston

My Sisters, Cheryl, Gerri, Joyce, and Debbie

Sharon

Corrine

Bri

Nakia

Donna

Betty

Rashideea

Tracey

Ellis

Carla

Meka

You've ALL encouraged and supported me through this whole journey. You've pushed me when I needed it, while loving me through it all. I thank you ALL for that.

PREFACE

Rachel stood in her best friend Lisa's bedroom, who also happened to be her Matron of Honor, admiring her reflection in the full-length mirror. Rachel wore a white wedding gown trimmed with lace and pearls that came slightly off the shoulder. She wondered what the pastor and her parents would say about the tattoo that she tried so hard to hide. It was a red heart that read "Baby girl" on her right shoulder.

"Oh well," she thought, "I tried," besides it's not like it's anything distasteful.

It was just the fact that it boldly showed that she defiled her TEMPLE!!! She giggled. But anyway, on to more happy thoughts, speaking of which, Rachel couldn't believe that after all these years, twelve to be exact, she was finally marrying the one man she'd loved since she could remember. She was tempted to pinch herself, except that if it were a dream she certainly didn't want to wake up.

Rachel had read so many books and seen many movies about women and men searching for that Mr. or Mrs. Right and living happily ever after, but she never really thought it would ever happen to her. When she remembered what it was like just a few years ago, she never would have believed that people could change, and change so drastically. She thought back to the day she'd left for the Navy. She'd never been away from her family before, and she was scared to death. Still, she was also very excited to see if she could make it on her own, without welfare. Yep, no more welfare checks, but also, no more Ra'Shaun.

Rachel had a three-year-old son whom she loved very dearly, and she couldn't imagine how she was going to get through the next week without him, let alone the next four years. Ra'Shaun was all she had, and besides her family, he was the only person that really loved her.

Rachel was originally supposed to leave for boot camp in October, but she'd recently been dumped by Wayne Wallis, and her heart was still trying to get over it. She and Wayne had been together for only three months, but Rachel felt... no one knew that what they shared was so much more than just some fling. They'd been best friends, but Wayne loved his daughter, and truth be told, he still had some very strong unresolved feelings for his daughter's mother. He decided to go back to her to try and make it work out, so they could be a real family.

Rachel wanted so badly to hate him for ripping her heart in two, but she couldn't because that was the kind of man he was and that was one of the reasons she fell so deeply in love with him. Rachel and Wayne broke up in March, after she'd gone over his house one night to find the other Rachel (that was his daughter's mother's name) lying across his chest while Wayne lying there in his boxers, Although nothing had happened and the other Rachel was fully clothed, Rachel still knew that it was over.

Wayne did the chivalrous thing and ran after her. They sat in his car and talked for about two hours just to end it. Rachel could hardly stand to be in the same town with him; it hurt so much. So, when her Recruiter called and told her that there was an opening for July and asked her if she wanted to wait until October or to leave in July, she jumped at the chance to get away.

As time revealed, the Navy turned out to be the best thing that had ever happened to her. She found herself there, she found her strength there, she found growth there, and most of all, she found Mitchell Ghram there.

CHAPTER ONE

The first time she saw him, she was working in the galley (Mess Cranking was what they called the 90-day tour every newly enlisted person had to take before they reported to their permanent working department). Rachel was serving the crew in the mess line when she looked up and saw this guy with the most beautiful green/brown eyes. He had a mole about the size of a dime on his right cheek. His hair was brown and wavy/curly. He was very bowlegged, and just beautiful to look at. Rachel gave him his burger and mashed potatoes and gravy; then, she handed him back his tray.

He said, "Thank you," and went on through the line.

Rachel wondered if he had a girlfriend. "Of course, he does," she thought. "Who in their right mind would let that one go unleashed."

Before she could finish her next thought, Hannah Sanchez came over and asked, "What time you get off today?"

"Two, why?" Rachel answered.

"Because I was gonna go do my laundry after work; you wanna come?" Hannah asked.

"Not really, but thanks anyway."

"Aw, come on Rachel. You don't never go nowhere, and I don't wanna go by myself," Hannah whined.

Rachel laughed and gave in, "Okay Hannah, but laundry and that's all, Shoot, I'm tired. Girl, this getting up at 4:30 in the morning is kicking my butt."

"Yeah, I know, but the good thing is when we go in at 5:00, we get off at 2:00, and that gives us time to do our laundry and get back in time to do whatever." Hannah said with a devious grin.

"Laundry...that's all!" Rachel insisted.

"Okay, okay laundry, that's all, Hannah echoed.

Rachel finished work about 2:15 and was waiting for Hannah in the barracks when she finally arrived around 2:30.

Hannah came in like a whirlwind as usual. She was about 4'11," and just made it into the Navy because you had to be at least 4'11." She had an hourglass figure. Her waist must have been about 26 inches; she had thick shoulder length hair. In fact, most of the guys on the ship wanted to get with her. That was until they learned what kind of music she liked, Hard Rock. Even Rachel thought it was funny that a sister so down with everything else was so out of touch with her roots as far as music went. Still, Hannah was a good friend. She and Rachel were in sister companies in boot camp and naturally became close friends after arriving to the same ship three weeks apart. They were the only people each other knew or trusted for that matter.

"Guess what," Hannah said. She was excited about something, and Rachel was almost afraid to ask what is was.

"What now, Hannah?" Rachel asked with a heavy sigh.

"Aw, don't even act all tired with me, Rachel," Hannah replied. "You know you need to get a real life. I mean all you do is work and sleep; shoot, if I didn't know better, I'd think you were pregnant, but I know that ain't true because you have to be touched by a man first." Hannah laughed.

Rachel laughed too because she knew Hannah was right.

Hannah continued, "Anyway... everybody from Deck is goin' to the Main Event tonight. Since it's our last weekend before we ship out to Cuba on Monday, you going?" Hannah searched Rachel's face to see if she could read what would be said, and as usual, she already knew the answer before Rachel could open her mouth.

"Hannah, I told you...laundry, nothing else. I'm tired," Rachel said.

"No, I'm tired of hearing you use the same excuse. Either you're tired, or you have a fiancée," Hannah said. Her was temper getting in the way of actually trying to help her friend to get off the ship to do more than just "laundry."

"Well, I do have a fiancée, and I am tired." Rachel could see where the conversation was going, and she wanted no part of trying to defend her relationship with Corey, a relationship she herself was beginning to question.

"Okay, you have a fiancée. Where is he, and how come ain't nobody seen him but you?"

Hannah was fed up with this Corey guy. Didn't he know that Rachel sat on that great big ship every day and night waiting for a letter or a phone call from him?

"If you ask me, you're too good for the punk. I see the ring on your finger, and I don't really believe you bought it yourself. no matter what everybody else says." Hannah said with a big grin,

Rachel laughed.

"Seriously though Rach, I'm not asking you to jump in the bed with someone else, I'm just asking you to enjoy your life. Where's the crime?" Hannah asked.

"Look, I know you mean well, and when we get back from Cuba, I promise, if you want to go to a club, I'll go with you," Rachel said.

"You mean it Rach?" Hannah asked hopefully.

"I promise; just don't be trying to get me to go to one of those clubs with all those white people and all that Hard

Rock music you be listening to on your Walkman, girl. That stuff will make somebody want to pull their hair out by the roots."

Rachel started moving her head like she was a head banger, and both ladies burst into laughter. They were still laughing when their cab pulled up to take them to the laundromat.

Later, when the cab pulled back up to the pier, the girls got out with their clothes and headed down the pier to their ship. Rachel looked up at the enormous vessel. She still got goosebumps when she realized that not only was this her home for the next four years, but it would be on the water headed to Cuba in just a few days. What was even more amazing than that was the fact that she was going to be on this big gray monster when it pulled away from the pier. She had no idea what was expected of her as far as her job went; she didn't know anything about being underway. Just the word alone was enough to scare the pants off of her. Rachel and Hannah flashed their Military I.D. cards as they walked onto the Quarter Deck of the USS KENNEDY AD 38. The officer of the deck smiled at them both; it was as if he knew they were new to the navy and to the ship. He could just see the awe in their eyes. When the girls got down three decks to their berthing (where they slept), they put their clothes away. Hannah tried one last time to get Rachel to go out with her, but to no avail. Rachel informed Hannah that she was going to catch a cab to a hotel, get a room, and forget, at least for the weekend, that she lived with 1400 other people on a big floating ship of which she still didn't know her way around. Rachel wondered just how long it would take her to learn her way around the ship. Some people said that it took them at least six months. The ship was so big; it was like a big floating town. One thing that made her feel better was knowing that Hannah didn't know any more about the ship than she did, even though she tried to impress Rachel and to make Rachel think that she had it going on.

"Oh, I get it. You got a man coming over to your room; don't you? Uh-huh, I got your number." Hannah said jokingly.

"Yeah right, I almost wish I did." Rachel admitted, and almost immediately wished she hadn't.

"Soooooo, come on to the Main Event with me, find yourself a man and bring him back here and take out all your sexual frustrations on him," Hannah coaxed.

"Don't start Hannah. I was just joking...kinda, but either way, I plan to watch me some T.V. all weekend long, order me some pizzas, watch cartoons Saturday morning, and just lounge around all by myself, so I will see you Monday morning."

"All right, all right, I won't try to convince you anymore," Hannah said finally defeated. "But, I might stop by to visit you if I get bored. What hotel you going to?" Hannah asked.

"Oh please, don't do me any favors." Rachel laughed.

"Oh, you know what I mean." Hannah corrected, and they both laughed. "So, where you gonna be?" Hannah asked.

"Probably at the Econo Lodge on Oceanview Ave, and feel free to come by and stay the night if you want. Just come alone, and don't tell anyone where I am," Rachel ordered.

Hannah mumbled something under her breath.

"I mean it Hannah. If you come, you better not come stepping up there with some knucklehead cause I ain't trying to be bothered," Rachel said.

"I got the point, Rach. I won't tell anybody your 'Classified Whereabouts.'" Hannah raised her right hand as she spoke and gave Hannah the sign for the Boy Scout's "Scout's Honor."

Rachel couldn't help but laugh. She knew she could count on Hannah to be true to her word, and she looked forward to spending time alone. Even as much as she loved spending time with her friend, Rachel just wanted to lick her wounds. She hadn't heard from Corey in over a month, and although she did wear his engagement ring, she feared the relationship had run its course. She had met Corey in Boot Camp. He was in her brother company, but they'd met when they both wound up on the Flag Drill Team during their Boot Camp tour. Corey was from South Bronx, NY, and he wore that fact on his chest like a medal. He also had a very bad temper; in the short eight months that he'd been in the Navy, he'd been to Captain's Mast at least twice and had been thrown in the brig for striking an officer. Rachel laughed as she thought about the one time she'd been to Captain's Mast. She was scared to death that she was going to get kicked out of the Navy before her career had even gotten off the ground. She had fallen asleep on watch and got caught. Fortunately, all she got was $150.00 taken from her check for two months. Shoot that hurt enough. Rachel's cab pulled into the hotel parking lot, and she got out, paid the cabbie, and went in to register. As soon as she signed in and received her room key, she ordered a pizza with everything but anchovies. When the pizza came, Rachel tipped the guy, grabbed a slice and a cold Dr. Pepper, and curled up on the big queen-sized bed to watch T.V. Rachel thought about her son, Ra'Shaun. She missed him so much. She promised herself that as soon as she got back from Cuba, she was going home to New Jersey to see her son and as much of her family as she could fit into one weekend. She laid down with her son on her mind, and soon, she was sleep. Even in her sleep, she really hoped that Hannah would not come to her hotel room that night.

CHAPTER TWO

Rachel made it to the ship just in time to get into her uniform and to make it to 7:30 a.m. muster. She was finally back in her permanent department which was deck. Deck department handled painting the ship, the paint locker, the Captain's Gig, any and all boats, the six cranes on deck, and of course, the very important driving of the ship itself. Rachel was standing next to Hannah who seemed to know quite a few people in the dept. Rachel was listening intently to the LPO (Leading Petty Officer) describe what had to be done before the ship could get underway for Cuba, who would be working with whom, where they would be working, and so on. Rachel was totally engrossed in what the LPO was saying (although she had no idea what it all meant) when Hannah whispered in her ear.

"Rachel, ain't Ghram cute?" She said in an excited whisper as if she had a secret that she couldn't wait to share.

"Who is Ghram?" Rachel asked.

"You know, Ghram, the one with the pretty eyes." Hannah was giggling like some stupid schoolgirl, and this early in the morning, Rachel was not in the mood.

"Hannah, I have no idea who or what a Ghram is," Rachel stated, getting annoyed. Didn't Hannah know how much she hated to leave her hotel room of no one but herself, to come to this great big ship to sleep in a rack about 6' by 3' in an isle about 3 across, with five other women in the same isle.

Rachel's mood didn't seem to dampen Hannah's one bit, "Look back; he's standing right behind you. God, he is so cute," Rachel thought that Hannah was actually starting to drool now.

So, she kind of half turned around and slyly looked over her shoulder. Rachel was surprised to see the same handsome guy who came through her line a few days ago, the one with the mole and the brown/green eyes. She was just about to turn back around and agree with Hannah on just how fine this Ghram guy was when he started laughing about something one of his friends said. Rachel couldn't believe that in just a mere second someone could go from "fine as hell" to "Oh my God" ugly.

Rachel turned back around and looked at Hannah who was anxiously awaiting her reply.

"Hannah, I thought he was cute til opened his mouth. Eeeww." Rachel said.

"You don't think he's cute? I think he's the cutest guy in the whole Deck Dept. I can't believe you don't think he's cute." Hannah said surprised.

"The cutest guy in the Dept? You must be crazy, Hannah. He look like a Barracuda with those big ole teeth and those big soup cooler lips." Rachel and Hannah both laughed.

"I still think he's fine," Hannah stated, still laughing.

"You would. Shoot, you think the Chief is cute, and he's old," Rachel was turning up her nose. "Hannah, you don't have the best taste." Rachel said.

"Aw you ain't gonna give anybody a chance anyway cause you still hung up on Corey," Hannah said.

"See, that's how much you know. I decided to end it with Corey," Rachel threw back. She couldn't believe she was admitting to Hannah that it was over. She hadn't really accepted it herself, but she knew it was best.

"Well, unless you went to Cuba and saw him this weekend, he still doesn't know. How do you plan to tell him. I know you not gonna do the classic Dear John letter," Hannah said with a funny look on her face.

"Well, how else am I supposed to tell him?" Rachel asked. "When he gets back, I'll be gone to Cuba, and by the time I get back, too much time will have passed. I have no other choice but to write him a letter." Rachel sounded defeated.

"Well, my question is, what's the big hurry? It's not like you're interested in someone else, Hannah baited.

"No, there is no one else that I'm interested in, but, and that's a very big but, if I did decide to see someone else, I wouldn't be cheating on Corey." Rachel said. She actually felt like she was bargaining with someone.

"Yeah right, like you really gonna give anybody else a chance." Hannah was still baiting.

"Well, why should I? From the moment I stepped foot on this big tuna boat, all the guys have been acting like they haven't eaten in six months, and I'm a walking T-Bone steak. Is that how they treat every girl who comes aboard?" Rachel asked.

"Yeah, and I'm glad. It's better than them treating us like dogs." Hannah stated.

"Oh, I see; you'd just rather them act like dogs." Rachel said with an attitude that she didn't understand. Hannah was the only friend she had and was only trying to make her feel more at ease, Rachel had no right to be so mean to her just because she was breaking up with Corey.

"I'm sorry," Rachel said. "I'm just tired." She lied. "Let's go find out who we're working with, and what we're doing."

"I hope we're working with Fulton. He don't make you do nothing, and that's just the kind of work I like." Hannah said grinning.

"I know that's right, especially when I have no idea what I'm doing, or where I'm going for that matter." Rachel said.

The girls walked over to the tool shack, retrieved their hard hats, and went to find out what was to become of them for the next eight hours.

It was now 12:00 p.m. Rachel and Hannah had been separated all morning. Hannah was lucky enough to get assigned to Fulton like she'd hoped, but Rachel had gotten stuck with Seaman Bowman, the last person with whom she wanted to be working. Reason one being that all he wanted to do was teach her how to skate (fake working) and that she didn't need, she was already lazy enough, and she didn't need any encouragement. Reason two was that Bowman had already made it clear that he was interested, but Rachel wasn't. Soon as they broke for lunch, Rachel ran for the berthing area. All she wanted was to jump into her rack, but she knew she couldn't. It was against the rules of the ship to be in your rack while in uniform, and you also weren't allowed to be in civilian clothes during hours. So, the first thing Rachel did was kick off her steel toe boots and lay on the floor right next to her rack. She had a bottom rack anyway, so it wasn't a big leap. Rachel was just starting to doze when she heard Hannah's familiar voice coming down the ladder. Hannah bounded over in her usual happy mood.

"Come on Rachel, ain't you gonna go eat?" she asked.

Rachel hesitated before lifting the ball cap off her face. Hannah obviously didn't get the hint that she didn't want to be disturbed. "I'm not hungry, but will you come back and wake me up when you get done?" Rachel said.

Hannah was not to be put off that easily, so she started her whining because she knew it would drive Rachel crazy. "Aw come on Rach, I don't want to go up on the Mess Deck by myself. I hate eating by myself." She cried.

"Oh God was she pouring it on thick," Rachel thought. "Okay Hannah, who is it that you're so hell bent on seeing topside?"

"Nobody," she said noticing the look on Rachel's face, "for real."

Rachel wasn't convinced, so she decided to call Hannah's bluff.

"All right, come on Hannah, but soon as you get done, we're coming right back down, so I can lay down before we go back up on deck." Rachel started for the ladder to go back up to the Mess Deck where the crew ate, but before she could put one foot on the first step, Hannah stopped her.

"Hold up a minute, Rach. I gotta go fix my hair and put on some more lip gloss." She said as she was going into the head.

When Hannah came out, Rachel was still standing at the bottom of the ladder waiting with a sly grin.

"What?" Hannah asked curiously.

"Who is he, Hannah?" Rachel asked with her arms folded across her chest.

"Nobody, Rachel, for real." Hannah was trying hard not to give herself away, but she knew no one could read her as well as her best friend.

Rachel started to tap her right foot in a way that always made Hannah laugh.

Hannah could hold it no longer. She finally broke into laughter, and so did Rachel. "Are you gonna tell me, or do I have to figure it out for myself?" Rachel asked.

"I told you. I'm just hungry, and I want a hamburger. Now, are you coming or not?" she replied.

Rachel decided to really put the pressure on her. "Not."

"Oh please, Rachel, I'll owe you one big, please, please, please." She begged.

Rachel couldn't help but laugh. "Okay, I was just messing with you. Come on, I need something to drink, but by the time lunch is over, I'll be able to tell you who it is that has you 'fixing your hair and putting on lip gloss' just to go eat a freakin' soy burger. They both laughed.

"Whatever you say, Rach, but I'm just trying to get something in my stomach since I missed breakfast." Hannah said.

"Mmm hmm, sure I believe you, Hannah." Rachel said sarcastically. The girls went up the ladder to the Mess Deck. Hannah got in line to get her burger that she was so hungry for, and Rachel just got something to drink. She went and sat down at an empty table and waited for her friend. Hannah finally came and sat down.

The girls had been sitting down for over twenty minutes when Rachel noticed that Hannah had yet to bite her hamburger. She kept looking across the room at another table with a lot of guys; some of which were in the same dept as them. Then, Rachel noticed that from that whole table of guys, only one of them seemed to be looking in their direction. Rachel played like she didn't notice anything. She just kept making small talk with her friend. Finally, just to get Hannah's goat, Rachel asked, "So Hannah, just out of curiosity, what did you do for a lunch partner before I got here?"

"I usually just sat by myself, or I might go over to McDonalds." She said not even looking at Rachel as she talked.

She was so engrossed in this guy that Rachel could have been talking about politics and Hannah wouldn't have known the difference.

"Well, I'm ready to go back down below; you ready?" Rachel asked. She'd already figured out who it was that Hannah liked, and she couldn't wait to rib her about it.

"Yeah, I guess." She said.

The girls got up. Hannah put her tray away, Rachel put her glass away, and back below they went. Hannah seemed like all the wind had just been let out of her sail. Rachel couldn't resist teasing her about her new interest.

"My God, Hannah, you don't have to look so glum. It's not like he's staying behind when the ship pulls out today. He's coming along with us, and you'll have two whole months to get to know him better."

"Who?" Hannah asked completely shocked that Rachel seemed to have figured out not only that she liked someone on the ship, but she acted like she knew exactly who it was.

As if reading her mind, Rachel said, "Yeah, I know exactly who Mr. 'Hamburger' is." Rachel started laughing so hard that Hannah had to join in. She knew there was no point in trying to play it off any longer; Rachel was just too smart for her.

"Okay, Rach, since you think you know so much, what's his name?" Hannah asked.

"Well, I only been in the dept a few days, so I don't know his name, but I can describe him to you." Rachel said confidently.

"Okay, go ahead," Hannah prodded.

"Okay, he's real tall and skinny, and brown skinned, and he has an okay smile." Rachel teased.

"Okay smile? Girl please, Evan is fine as..." suddenly Hannah caught herself, but it was too late. Rachel was already smiling like the cat that had just swallowed the canary.

"And does this Evan have a last name?" Rachel asked.

"You'll never guess," Hannah said about to burst with pride.

"Well I'm sure I won't since I don't know anyone on the whole ship except you." Rachel stated.

"Oh...right, well anyway his name is Evan Sanchez." Hannah was smiling so hard that Rachel was expecting to be picking little pieces of Hannah off the wall any second now. Hannah literally looked like she was gonna explode with pride.

"Get outta here; you guys actually have the same last name?" Rachel herself was even taken aback.

"Evan says that I was stationed on this ship so that I would be his wife, and he's gonna marry me someday." She was actually beaming.

"Ooooh, how original, boy he sounds like a real catch; better not let that one get away." Rachel was starting to feel the green-eyed monster beginning to creep into the situation, and the last thing she wanted was to dump on her friend just because she and Corey were breaking up.

"I'm sorry, Hannah. I'm just jealous because of the situation with me and Corey. I'm glad you found someone to put a smile that big on your pretty face; you deserve it.

"It's okay. I know you didn't mean it." Hannah said, but it still did sting a little that Rachel would put down someone who was important to her when she didn't even give him a chance. It just wasn't like Rachel. That was it. Hannah decided she was going to find someone for her girl if it killed her, though it just might kill Rachel to let her guard down and let someone in. At least she'd die a happy death, Hannah smiled to herself.

CHAPTER THREE

"Underway, shift colors."

Rachel couldn't believe that the giant ship she was standing on was actually pulling away from the pier. It didn't even seem real. The people and cars on the pier seemed to get smaller and smaller. Hannah came over and stood by her side, and they were both in awe. They felt like little girls watching the circus come to town. They couldn't stop smiling. The farther they got into the channel, the greener the water became. It was supposed to take them three or four days to get to Cuba. Rachel didn't know what to expect or how to act. She didn't want to act like it was no big deal that she was, right now, floating on a ship to another country. Except for boot camp and now being in Norfolk, VA, she'd never been anywhere before, at least not alone without her family. Being the youngest in the family, she realized that she'd led a fairly sheltered life. Now, she was about to, through the Navy, see the world. She couldn't wait.

Hannah had said something that brought Rachel out of her daydream.

"What did you say, Hannah?" Rachel asked reluctantly coming back down to earth.

"I asked you if you had a watch today." She said.

"Yeah, I have the next watch at 3:45 to 5:45." Rachel answered.

"You mean the 1600 to 1800." Hannah corrected. "You better start learning the lingo; some of these officers can be a trip. They'll give you an extra watch just for saying floor or something like that." Hannah said.

"Okay, if it's not a floor, then what in the world is it?" Rachel asked.

"A deck." Hannah said. "You know what, we still got a couple of hours before your watch. How about we go over some of the terms when we get down stairs?"

"Thanks, Hannah, I sure appreciate it, but don't you mean 'down below?'" Rachel laughed.

"See, you getting the hang of it already."

"I ain't gonna lie; the hardest part for me was learning the times. All that 1400 this and 1900 that, shoot I wasn't that good in math; now, I have to learn how to tell time in a whole different way." Hannah complained. Both girls laughed.

"God, Hannah, I still can't believe were floating; it doesn't even feel like we're moving." Rachel said.

"I know. I hope I don't get sick." Hannah said.

"I never thought about that. I guess if I was gonna get sick, I would know by now." Rachel thought aloud.

"Rachel, who are you standing watch with?" Hannah asked.

She knew it had to be someone from deck, and if it were someone cute, Hannah planned to play matchmaker.

"I don't know. How do I find out?" Rachel asked.

"You have to go the deck office and find out. You want me to go with you?" Hannah was anxious to find out herself;

she needed to know with what she was gonna have to work.

"Would you? I ain't even sure where it is." Rachel admitted.

"No problem, I'll tell you what; let's kill two birds with one stone. Let's take a tour around the ship, and while we do that, we'll work on your Navy vocabulary, cool?' Hannah asked.

"Cool!" Rachel said. "Thanks for looking out for me, even though I have been the Big B lately." Rachel said.

"You'll understand if I don't argue with you about that, right?" Hannah said smiling. "Now, even though it's not that important as far as your job goes, the most important place you need to know is the ship's store." Hannah stated.

"We actually have a store onboard this ship?" Rachel asked unbelievingly.

"Of course, we do. =Where else are we gonna get our Tampons from?' Hannah asked. The girls both laughed.

Rachel still had trouble wrapping her mind around the fact that she was floating out in the great big ocean on a giant piece of metal, and they weren't sinking. Now, she finds out that there was actually a store somewhere inside this big metal fish!

"What was next," she thought, "a gymnasium?"

Sure enough, after the store, Hannah took Rachel to the Crew's lounge which actually had a gym inside. Hannah kept laughing at the reactions she was getting from Rachel, remembering all the while how she had the same reactions when she saw the whole ship for the first time. The only difference was, that she had to find everything on her own. Hannah noticed that Rachel was a little reluctant to go out and learn the ship or even the people by herself, but Hannah was going to change that if she could because she had found out that being by herself on a vessel this large was a scary thing, and she wouldn't wish that on anyone, especially her best friend.

While Rachel was getting ready for her watch, Hannah was silently laughing inside. She knew who Rachel was going to be standing watch with, and she was wishing she could be a fly on the "bulkhead" when Rachel saw who it was. The watch bill had Rachel down as "UI"(Under Instruction), which meant the other person standing watch with her would actually be instructing her. So, there was actually going to be the person teaching Rachel, plus one other person on watch with her. One of those people, Hannah knew for a fact, was Frank Cavanaugh. Frank had been asking Rachel out since she had boarded the ship, but Rachel kept turning him down saying he was too young. Frank was only 19, and Rachel was 23. Hannah had gotten her info from Evan who slept in the same berthing area with the guys, and Rachel just happened to be a hot topic down there especially since no one had been lucky enough to claim her yet. Evan had told Hannah that he'd heard Ghram had paid to take someone else's watch so that he could stand watch with Rachel. He didn't even have a watch, but he didn't want Frank to be alone with Rachel. They were both determined not to let the other get a foot in the door.

"What in the world are you looking at me like that for, and why are you smiling?" Rachel asked, suddenly very suspicious of Hannah, not knowing the guys with whom Rachel was going to be standing watch. "Well, whoever it was, she just hoped it wasn't some lifer who just wanted to talk Navy all night." Rachel thought.

"Dang, a person can't be happy anymore?" Hannah said, still smiling.

"I know one thing," Rachel said, "I better not be walking into no mess."

"What are you talking about girl? I don't make up the watch bill." Hannah insisted.

"You heard what I said. Huh, I know what rack you sleep in, you little munchkin." Rachel teased.

"See, you ain't right, especially when you only got me by 2 inches, which only makes you about 5'1." Hannah said.

"I am a very tall, 5'3" thank you very much." Rachel said with pride.

"Yeah right, in munchkin land." Hannah laughed.

"Well anyway, I'm just glad it's only a 2-hour watch cause I can't wait to get in my rack, turn on my walkman, and get all into "Kenny G." Rachel said.

Hannah rolled her eyes upward. "Oh my God, Rach, you get off watch at 19:45; it probably won't even be dark by then, and you talking about going to bed. You really need to find yourself a man." Hannah said.

"Speaking of man, who is BM2 Brown anyway?" Rachel asked remembering that she still didn't know with whom she was standing watch. Well, she knew Frank, but she didn't know Brown. Somehow Hannah seemed to know it all when it came to the Deck Dept. men, courtesy of Evan Sanchez no doubt.

"Oh, he just some Redneck, no big deal." Hannah stated just a little too nonchalantly.

"Okay, that's it!" Rachel slammed down her hairbrush. "What the hell are you not telling me Hannah? I'm serious."

Hannah could tell that she was serious, so she came clean. She told Rachel that she'd heard that Ghram didn't have a watch and took BM2 Brown's watch just so he could stand watch with her and block Frank at the same time.

Rachel was appalled, furious, and truth be told, a little flattered. But of course, she couldn't let Hannah know this, not yet anyway.

"God, men make me sick," Rachel nearly yelled, faking exasperation.

"Better watch your mouth girlfriend; there's plenty of women down here that might take that statement as an open invitation." Hannah laughed.

"Eeewww, you nasty," Rachel said with an upturned nose.

"I might be nasty, but you still better watch your mouth before you find yourself pinned-up against a wall somewhere. And I'm telling you right now, you my girl and all, and you know I love you to death, but if one of these big *heffers* act like they want to get busy with you, I'm gone." Hannah said laughing.

"Dang, Hannah, it's bad enough to be ogled over by Frank every five minutes, but now Ghram too. I mean, damn, don't anybody try to get to know a girl just because they're curious about what's she's like?" Rachel asked.

"Sure they do; then, after they find out what you're like, they want to find out what you're like 'in bed.'" Hannah said with a smile.

"That's just it, Hannah. I'm tired of being treated like a piece of meat." Rachel whined," "That's all men want!"

"Okay, now, I have to stop you. So, you're saying that all men are the same, and they only want one thing and so on. Well, you're stereotyping them just like you say they're doing you. Besides, Frank and Mitchell are both nice guys. They ain't like that; they both just happen to like the same girl. All they want 'is' to get to know you, and you're freaking out." Hannah said.

"Boy, did the truth hurt," Rachel thought." "I got to go. I don't want to be late for my first watch." Rachel said.

"It's all right Rach, I know it hurts, but I got some Band-Aids in my rack if you need one." Hannah said.

"What hurts?" Rachel asked not having a clue that she was yet again the butt of one of her friend's jokes.

"The truth!" Hannah said.

"Oh, shut up!" Rachel said as she threw her ball cap at Hannah and went on up the ladder to stand her watch. "This is going to be interesting," she thought. She stopped along the way looking in every mirror she could to make sure that every hair was in place and that her uniform was just so. She checked her boots to make sure they shined perfectly. She smelled her wrists to see if she could still smell her perfume. Rachel knew that the officers didn't play, and she wanted to look her best just in case the Captain came on the bridge.

"Yeah right," she thought. "For the Captain, come on Rachel," she said to herself aloud. "Even you don't believe that one." She smiled to herself as she stepped onto the bridge.

CHAPTER FOUR

Rachel was completely amazed and intimidated by all the lighted panels she saw when she stepped into the room. At first, she had to let her eyes adjust because it was still very sunny outside, but the Bridge area was kept especially dark. Most of the lighting came from the lighted panels themselves. Rachel spotted Frank right away which was probably because she could feel someone was staring at her. Frank really was a nice guy and was even very cute, but there was just something about him that seemed so immature. Other than that, she probably would have given him a chance. Nevertheless, he came at her every chance he got and that was just a turn off in Rachel's book.

Rachel watched as Frank walked over to her. He really was cute, kind of short, but very cute. He could stand to lose about five or ten pounds, but she couldn't really call him fat. Rachel was preparing herself for the come on she knew was coming and had to admit that she was pleasantly surprised when it didn't.

"Hey Tiegs," Frank said. "Is this your first watch?" He asked.

"Hey, Frank," Rachel said. "Yeah, I never stood watch before. Okay, unless you count the one time I stood watch in boot camp and fell asleep."

"Well don't be falling asleep up here, unless you wanna go to Captain's Mast." Frank Joked. He could tell Rachel was nervous, and he wanted to make her feel more at ease.

"Come on, Tiegs, I'll take you out on the Portside and explain everything to you." Frank said.

"First of all, call me Rachel; second, what in the world is a Portside?" Rachel asked.

Frank laughed. "That's what you call the left side of the ship."

"So why don't they just say the left side of the ship?" Rachel asked jokingly.

"I don't know Rachel, but I'll ask the Captain when I see him." Frank said, and they both laughed.

Frank explained everything about the Bridge that pertained to Deck personnel. He told her about the Helm and that it was actually the steering wheel of the ship. She also learned about the Lee Helmsmen and that they were the people who took the order from the Officer of the Deck on how fast the ship was to go and gave that same order to the Engine room.

It was all so fascinating. Frank told Rachel that she would spend half the watch on Portside and the other half on Starboard side. Frank seemed to be a different person on watch than the person who was always begging for a date. Rachel was impressed by the way he carried himself on the Bridge. She also appreciated the fact that he was actually concentrating on teaching her what she needed to know about the ship and not treating her like she was a piece of steak after not having a bite to eat in month.

After a half an hour on the Bridge, Frank took Rachel outside on the Portside and explained to her how the Port and Starboard Watch are responsible for reporting anything they see anywhere out on the horizon or closer. He handed her the binoculars, so she could take a look at the surrounding area. Rachel looked at the ocean from the two small windows of the binoculars. It seemed so vast and beautiful. She could see a ship far off in the distance. Rachel knew that she didn't have to report this particular ship because it had already been reported by the previous watch, so the Officer of the Deck was aware of its presence. There was also an aircraft carrier out on the Starboard side.

"Is that aircraft carrier out there a US ship?" Rachel asked after studying the vessel through the binoculars for a few minutes.

"Yeah," Frank answered, "That's the USS Kennedy. We're part of the same battle group."

"What's a battle group?" she asked.

"That's a group of ships that usually deploy together." Frank told her.

"Have you ever been on a carrier?" Rachel asked, hoping that she wasn't asking too many questions, but there was so much she wanted to know. It was all just so exciting to her.

"Nah, I mean I took a tour of one, but I've never been stationed on one. I've only been in the navy just under two years." Frank said.

"Really, I thought you been in longer than that. You seem to know your way around pretty good I mean."

"It don't take long to learn your way around." Frank said.

"Yeah, that's what Hannah keeps saying." Rachel said.

"No, for real, it won't take you long at all." Frank thought for a minute; then, he asked a little shyly, "You want me to show you around?"

"Thanks Frank, I appreciate it, but Hannah is gonna show me around. But thanks for offering." Rachel said surprised to see Frank showing his shy side. "He really was a nice guy," she thought.

After a while, Frank took Rachel back over on the Starboard side where Ghram was. All of a sudden, Rachel was nervous. Frank left, and Rachel felt like she'd just been left on a blind date. Still, just like Frank, Ghram explained to Rachel everything she needed to know about standing watch on the Starboard side.

Also, just like Frank, Ghram seemed to be concentrating on the task of teaching her instead of trying to get to know her personally. At some point, but Rachel couldn't remember when, Ghram became Mitchell, then Mitch, and before Rachel knew it, she and Mitch were talking about everything but what goes on while standing watch. She felt like she'd known him for years.

Rachel told Mitch about Ra'Shaun, and her family at home in Jersey. Mitch told her about his girlfriend back at home in Ohio. Rachel was surprised to find out that his girlfriend was white. Mitch was 19 and his parents only son.

Mitch, like Frank, was easy to talk to and seemed very nice.

Before they knew it, the watch was over. Mitch showed Rachel how to turn the watch over to the next person. He also told Rachel that they had watch together again the next night, but it would be a four hour watch instead of two hours. Rachel told him that she would see him at work the next day. She left the Bridge and went on down to her berthing. She couldn't wait to get out of her uniform and into her pajamas. Of course, that was not to happen without a game of twenty questions from Hannah who happened to be waiting for Rachel by her rack smiling.

"Oh God, here we go!" Rachel said exasperated. "What do you want to know Hannah?" Rachel asked.

"How was your watch?" Hannah asked hopefully.

"It was fine; I learned a lot." Rachel decided to make Hannah beg for details. "For instance, I learned that there are over five thousand people on an aircraft carrier, and did you know that this ship couldn't get underway without Deck personnel? I had no idea that we were so important to the Navy, much less the ship." Rachel went on.

"Would you give me a break, Rach? I know all that; it didn't excite me when I learned it then, and it still don't get me hot now." Hannah said getting impatient with Rachel.

Rachel could barely keep her composure. "Really, I thought all that stuff about Portside and Starboard side, and the Officer on the Deck, and oh, I saw some dolphins and..."

"First of all," Hannah interrupted, "It's Officer 'of' the Deck, and second of all, I see fish all the time. Now, will you stop playing, and tell me what happened on watch?" Hannah asked now laughing along with Rachel who could hold it no longer.

"Okay, okay, well, don't get a big head, but you were right. Both the guys are very nice and much fun to look at. They didn't even try to get with me." Rachel said a little deflated.

Hannah didn't miss the note of disappointment in her friend's voice. She actually thought it was funny that it only took one hour with each of the guys to change Rachel's mind about them.

"Hold up, are you telling me that Frank and Mitch didn't pull out a steak knife and fork and devour you the moment you walked on the bridge?" Hannah asked with her eyes opened wide like she was surprised.

Rachel laughed. "Whatever."

Hannah noticed that Rachel was getting into her pjs. "I know you ain't going to bed already. It's only 8:30." She said.

"Actually, it's 20:30." Rachel said with a sarcastic smile. "And yes, I'm going to get into my rack with my book and my man, Kenny G."

"You're not gonna go to the crew's lounge and watch the movie with me?" Hannah whined.

"Girl, I gotta get some sleep. I can't be going on watch tomorrow with no bags under my eyes." Rachel said.

"Oh my God, now you care how you look on watch. I wonder why." Hannah said laughing. "Girl please, your watch ain't til 8'oclock tomorrow night." Hannah stated.

"Again, it's 20 hundred hours." Rachel corrected.

"Whatever Rachel, either way, it's gonna be pitch black on the bridge and outside where you'll be standing watch." Hannah threw back.

"Well anyway, I've seen Top Gun a million times, and although it is one of my favorites, I'll pass tonight." Rachel said. "It's been a long day, and I really am tired."

"All right, I'll leave you alone for now. I'm satisfied with the fact that you had to admit that I was right and that the guys are nice, not to mention fine as all outdoors." Hannah said smiling.

"I'll see you in the morning; you going to breakfast with me?" Hannah asked.

"Yeah, I'll go to 'Chow' with you in the morning." Rachel corrected; she was beginning to like this new language.

"Lord, I done created a damn monster." Hannah walked away laughing. She thought it was so hilarious that just earlier that day Rachel didn't think that she was ever going to learn the Navy lingo. Now, she's talking the yang better some of the ole' dogs that have been on the ship for years. Of course, if she was to bring this small fact to her friend's attention, she would go to her grave denying it. Again, Hannah had to laugh. She hoped that between Mitch, Rachel, and Frank that two of the three would become a couple. "Lord, I hope it don't wind up being

Mitch and Frank." Hannah laughed, but she'd seen her share of strange couples on the ship in just the short time she'd been there.

Hannah went on down to the crew's lounge to watch the movie; she knew Evan would wonder what happened to her if she didn't show up. She couldn't wait to tell him about the different Rachel that came back from a 2-hour watch. She also knew that once she told Evan about Rachel's reaction to Mitch and Frank, he would go back, tell the guys, and the race would begin.

It had been two weeks since the USS Pennington had pulled into Cuba. The crew had worked normal hours as usual, but during the day, at least two or more drills would be run.

These drills would consist of anything from fire drills and chemical warfare, to what to do if the ship was hit by hostile fire. The worst part was all drills were done with all the power on the ship cut off and most of the ship in darkness. None of the crew had been allowed liberty yet. So, no one had been off the ship. The USS Pennington had to pass all of her drills and inspections in order to be allowed to go back to the States, and no one would step foot on land until this task was completed. The ship was expected to complete all drills and inspections in about three more weeks. Rumor had it that The USS Pennington was passing with flying colors.

Rachel, Hannah, Frank, and Mitch were out on the Boat Deck working together on the crane tracks. The heat was almost unbearable. It had been over 100 degrees for the past six days alone. Rachel didn't seem to notice the heat much; she was so happy just being with her friends.

Their assignment for the day was to clean all the grease from the crane tracks. Afterward, they had to re-lubricate the tracks with fresh grease so that the cranes would move across them more smoothly.

Rachel and Mitch had become close over the past few weeks. Everyone seemed to think that they were a couple, but the two always said, "Nah, we're like brother and sister."

Rachel would always say that Mitch was four years younger than her and that when they were together all, they talked about was his girlfriend, Becca (Rebecca).

Mitch had recently told Rachel that he'd gotten a girl pregnant back in Norfolk. He said that it was just a one-night stand although she had wanted it to be more. Her name was Melissa. Mitch told Rachel that he and Melissa had agreed that while he was in Cuba, Melissa would get an abortion. He had given her the money before he left for Cuba, and the appointment was already made. Mitch felt that his problems in Norfolk would be solved when he returned in a few weeks.

Rachel wasn't so sure. First of all, his girlfriend back at home didn't know anything about Melissa, much less about a baby on the way. Rachel wondered how Becca would feel. For some reason, it seemed to bother Rachel more than she was willing to admit to Mitch or herself. Rachel was so deep in thought that she didn't hear Hannah talking to her.

"Hello, earth to Rachel!" Hannah yelled practically into Rachel's ear, bringing her out of her deep thought.

"I'm sorry, Hel; what did you say?" Rachel asked.

"I said, I heard we're supposed to be having a drill right before chow." She repeated.

"Aw man," Rachel whined, "I hope not; every time we have a drill before chow time, the food be all cold and nasty."

"Girl please, the food be nasty anyway." Hannah said laughing. The guys agreed.

"Yo, we need some more brushes. Why don't one of you go and get a few more from the tool shed?" Frank said.

"What we look like, your maids? Go get it yourself." Hannah shot back.

"Oh, here we go, Mitch," Frank sighed," Now, they gonna get all feminine on us."

Mitch laughed, "Man I ain't got nothing to do with what ya'll talking about."

"Oh, okay, you just gonna leave a brother out here all by hisself." Frank said faking anger.

"Nah man, it ain't even like that." Mitch was laughing. "But you know they can be over sensitive sometime; you might want to ask them instead of ordering them." Mitch explained with a wink.

"Thank you, Mitch," Hannah said sarcastically. "All you had to do was ask nicely.........like this. Rachel, go get some more brushes." Hannah ordered.

"Yeah right," Rachel said laughing. "I don't advise you to wait for me to go get some brushes."

"You know I'm just kidding," Hannah laughed.

"I know," Rachel said as she got up and began to run and jump over the track on which they were working. Just as she thought she'd cleared the track with her left leg, she heard a resounding crack.

Rachel felt a sharp pain in her left knee. She was only a few feet from the tool shed so she hobbled over to the door. Seaman Melissa Dolan was in charge of the tool shed for the week. Melissa was also good friends with Hannah and Rachel. She'd witnessed Rachel whacking her knee on the track. She could see the pain etched across Rachel's face. She looked like she was going to pass out.

"Rachel, are you all right?" Melissa asked, "I know that hurt; I heard it all the way over here." Melissa said concerned.

"Yeah, I'm all right; I just need to sit down for a minute." Rachel said trying to be strong, but she didn't really believe it herself. She could feel her knee already swelling quickly.

She remembered what she came to the tool shed to get.

"Lissa, I need four more brushes for the track." Rachel said through clinched teeth.

Melissa left and came back with the brushes. She could see that Rachel's knee was swollen through her dungaree pants.

"Rachel, you need to go to sick call. I can see your knee is swollen through your pants." Melissa said.

"I'll be all right; Rachel lied. She tried to stand, but as soon as she put her weight on her left knee, she fell back down. Melissa helped her to sit down.

"I'm gonna go get Fulton." Melissa said. She left to go and get the LPO (Leading Petty Officer) Fulton. Melissa and Fulton had been a couple for months now, but they had to be careful because Fulton was her boss. They could get in trouble for fraternizing.

"Rachel, I thought you were getting the brushes." Hannah said as she walked up. "I knew you and Melissa was over here running off at the mouth." Hannah suddenly got quiet when she saw the pain on her friend's face; then she noticed her holding her knee.

"What happened, Rachel?" Hannah asked.

"Remember when I went to jump over the track to go to the tool shed?" Rachel asked.

"Yeah." Hannah said waiting to hear about whatever must have happened right in front of her, and she still managed to miss it.

"Well, you know me 'Clumsy Smurf.' I didn't lift my left knee high enough." Rachel said embarrassed. "I can't put my weight on it." Rachel told her friend. She was really starting to get scared now.

Hannah could hear the fear in Rachel's voice, and it was very noticeable on her face. She felt she should say something to calm her.

"Don't worry, Rach; you'll be all right. You're tougher than that rusty ole' track." Hannah said smiling, but she was worried herself because she could see how swollen Rachel's leg was.

Melissa came back with Fulton. He took one look at Rachel's leg and called down to sick bay.

"Tiegs, you just sit tight until Medical gets here." Fulton instructed.

By this time, Mitch and Frank noticed that not only had Rachel not come back with the brushes, but Hannah was missing too.

"They probably off somewhere skating." Frank said to Mitch as they were both walking over to the tool shed. As they got closer, they both realized something was going on because everybody in deck was at the tool shed and so was Medical.

Just as the guys were stepping up to the tool shed, they heard over the "One MC," "Medical emergency on the Boat Deck, repeat medical emergency on the Boat Deck."

Before the guys could see who or what the medical emergency was, the Medical Personnel were pushing their way through crowd.

"Make a hole people," one guy said, not too nicely. They had a stretcher with them. When Rachel saw the stretcher, she had to fight down the panic rising within her. She wanted to run, except she couldn't even walk. She wished she could crawl under one of the boats and hide. Everyone was gawking at her like she was some little wounded bird. Suddenly she heard the word "broken."

"What did you say?" Rachel asked wide eyed. "It can't be broken. I didn't hit it that hard." She protested.

"It's better to be safe than sorry; besides, we won't know if it's broken til we get you to the hospital and get some x-rays." The nicer corpmen informed Rachel. He could see how distressed she was, and he hoped to calm her. Nonetheless, Rachel just wanted to rewind back the last hour and tell Mitch and Frank to go and get their own brushes.

The corpmen helped Rachel onto the stretcher. She felt so helpless lying there flat on her back with everyone looking down at her. Then, as the crown cleared to let the corpmen through, everyone's eyes were on her, but all she saw was Mitch. He couldn't get near her because the crowd was so large, but he smiled and winked at her, and suddenly she forgot her embarrassment, her fear, and she almost forgot her pain.

She felt that he was telling her to be strong and that everything would be all right.

Rachel was placed on a boat and taken to land where an ambulance was waiting to take her to the hospital. Her fear was returning as she realized that if her knee was broken, she might need surgery. She didn't want American doctors cutting on her leg, much less Cuban doctors. What if they opened up the wrong leg, or worse, what if they opened up something other than a leg?. She began to pray silently to herself. "Funny," she thought, "You don't talk to Him until you're in trouble, or you want something." She felt sad and ashamed. "Forgive me," she said quietly. Rachel was lifted into the ambulance and taken to the hospital. Soon, she would know just how much damage she'd done.

CHAPTER FIVE

Rachel sat on the edge of her hospital bed sulking. She wanted so badly to go to the ship and see her friends. She especially couldn't wait to see Mitch. She'd been at the hospital for two weeks now. Today, she was supposed to find out if she would be able to go back to the ship or go back to the states and wait for the ship to return.

Although she wanted to go back Virginia, she didn't want to go back alone. She had been told by one of the hospital corpsmen that the USS Pennington had failed a couple of drills and that because of this the ship would be thrown back at least two weeks. Fortunately, Rachel had only suffered a hairline fracture on her left kneecap. She didn't need surgery, and only had to wear a soft leg cast for four weeks.

While Rachel was a patient, she was actually considered stationed at the hospital, so she had to work half days in the records room filing charts. Her hours were from 0800 in the morning to 1200 in the afternoon.

It was now after twelve in the afternoon, and Rachel was bored as usual. She picked up the T.V. remote and searched through the channels for what must have been the hundredth time. All the channels were in Spanish, and it was driving her crazy watching the Young and the Restless, and not having a clue what was being said.

Rachel turned off the T.V. and grabbed her book she started to read the night before. It wasn't long before she heard voices, familiar voices. She looked up to see Fulton and Melissa standing in her doorway. Rachel had never been so happy to see familiar faces, not to mention talk to someone and have them understand what she was saying.

"Hey Tiegs." Fulton said smiling. He had a very friendly smile, and it reflected exactly the kind of sweet honest guy he was.

"Hey Fulton." Rachel said grinning back at the two of them. "What's up Melissa?"

Melissa bent down to give Rachel a hug. "We miss you, Rach. When they gonna let you go home?" She asked.

"I'm supposed to find out today." Rachel answered.

"Hey Tiegs, don't tell him I told you this, but Ghram, been pitiful since you left." Fulton said laughing. "I think you got his head." He added.

"Now, if that was me that told you that Rach, he would have told me to stay out of it." Melissa said with indignation. "So, I'm gonna tell you; stay out of it Fulton."

All three laughed. "So, Rach, are you going back to the states, or are they gonna make you come back to the ship?" Melissa asked.

"I don't know; that's what I'm waiting to find out. I hope I get to come back to the ship. I don't want to go back to Norfolk by myself. The doctor is here somewhere. I guess he'll tell me one way or the other." Rachel said.

"Man, if it was me, I would run back to the states." Fulton said.

"Oh, you telling me you would just leave me here?" Melissa asked faking hurt feelings.

"With the quickness babe, but I would be waiting for you on the pier when the ship pulled back in." Fulton said trying to do damage control.

"Yeah, I bet." Melissa said.

Melissa was probably the prettiest white girl in Deck Dept. She had short brown hair, an olive complexion, and big hazel eyes. She almost made you think of a beautiful doe. It was obvious that she and Fulton were very close, but Melissa was the tomboy type, and she never mentioned the "L" word when she spoke about Fulton.

Fulton on the other hand wore his heart on his sleeve. He was about six feet tall, the classic blonde hair, blue eyed hunk. "He and Melissa made a handsome couple." Rachel thought to herself.

"So, you want to come back to the ship, Rach? Why?" Melissa asked already knowing the answer. She knew just how close Mitch and Rachel had become, even if they wouldn't admit it.

"I don't want to be in Virginia by myself." Rachel said.

"But you would be on shore duty til the ship gets back." Melissa argued. "Besides, you could go home to Jersey on the weekend; you said you're only four hours from home."

"Yeah, I know, but I still would rather go back with the ship." Rachel said wishing Melissa would drop the subject.

"Okay, you're saying you would rather come back to the ship where it's hot as hell and dark when we're in the middle of drills, than go back to the states where the weather is beautiful? You would stay in the barracks with probably one other person instead of hundreds."

"Yeah, Lissa, I want to stay here!" Rachel said hoping that Melissa could hear the "drop it" in her voice.

"Okay, just wanted to be sure that's what you really wanted." Melissa baited with a smile.

"Besides, I don't think it's up to me whether I stay or go." Rachel said.

"That's true." Fulton agreed.

Just then, a man whom Rachel assumed was the doctor walked into the room. Rachel was glad Melissa's attention was on something else besides her personal life.

"Are you Seaman Tiegs?" He asked Rachel. He had a very strong accent, but Rachel understood him. He was tall, dark, and very handsome with beautiful white teeth.

"Yes sir." Rachel answered.

"You don't have to call me sir; I'm a civilian." He said smiling. "My name is Dr. Quienonez, and I'm handling your case. Were you told that you have a hairline fracture on your left kneecap?"

"Yes, I was." Rachel said she was starting to get nervous.

"Well, fortunately you won't need surgery, but you whacked your leg pretty good." He said.

"Yeah, I know; I was there. I can't believe how clumsy I was." She said embarrassed.

"I'm putting you on light duty for the next three weeks, and I want you wear the soft cast whenever you put your weight on the leg." He gave Rachel verbal orders as he was writing in her chart.

"Do you have any questions for me, Seaman Tiegs?" He asked when he finished writing.

She was afraid to ask, but she had to know. So, she just blurted out. "How much longer do I have to stay here?"

"Well actually, you can be discharged today." He said still smiling.

"Today? Really?" Rachel couldn't believe her ears. And then it hit her, and she thought, "Discharged to where, the ship or the states?"

Doctor Quienonez saw Rachel's smile suddenly fade as she went into a deep thought. "Is something wrong, Seaman Tiegs?" He asked concerned for his patient.

"Well, yeah, where am I being discharged to?" She asked almost afraid to hear the answer.

"Well, that's up to you." He said.

"You mean if I want to go back to my ship? I don't 'have' to go back to the states if I don't want to?" Rachel asked amazed at her luck.

"Yes, you decide, not your command unless of course you became a safety hazard to the ship because of the soft cast. But I'll make the recommendation the you return to the ship immediately, if you like." He said.

"Oh, would you please? I really don't want to go back to the states without my ship." Rachel said.

"No problem, but don't forget, no weight on that leg without the soft cast for three weeks, promise?" He said.

"Promise." Rachel said. "And thank you so much."

"I'll go and get started on your discharge. You should be ready to leave in a couple of hours." He said as he walked out of the room.

"Well Tiegs, we were sent over here by the Captain to check on all the people from our command, but since you're being discharged, we might as well wait for you." Fulton said. "I'll go and check on the other three people we have here and then I'll be back to see if you're ready, okay?"

"Okay, I'll be ready; believe me." Rachel said rising off the bed as she spoke.

"I'll stay here and help Rachel get packed." Melissa said.

"All right, I'll be right back." Fulton said; then, he left.

Fulton's shadow hadn't even fully rounded the corner before Melissa pounced.

"I can't believe you want to come back to the ship instead of going back to the states." Melissa said. "What's wrong with you, Rach? You could go home and see your family."

"Melissa, please don't start. I don't want to go back. Besides, if I do, what have I learned? We came here to learn specific things about Damage Control and to pass certain inspections. If I leave now, I haven't learned anything except how to scrub grease off of a damn crane track." Rachel said as her voice raised an octave.

Melissa knew Rachel well enough to know to let it alone, but not without one last stab.

"Okay fine, but at least be honest with yourself. If you want to stay to learn more about 'Damage Control' (she mocked the quote sign with her fingers), that's all good and well, but admit the fact that Mitch has something to do with your decision too."

"Okay Lissa, if it'll get you off my back, I'll admit that I miss 'my friend' (Rachel mocked Melissa with the quote sign), Mitch, but no more than I miss Hannah or you for that matter." Rachel reasoned.

"All right, all right, Rach, that's your story and evidently you're sticking to it." Melissa said smiling. "And you know what, just to show you that I only want what's gonna make you happy, I'm not even gonna say 'I told you so' when the time comes."

"Whatever Lissa." Rachel said smiling also to let Melissa know that she wasn't mad.

The girls were just finishing up Rachel's packing when Fulton returned. He told them that the other three people weren't being discharged yet. One still needed surgery, and the other two still had yet to see the doctor.

Shortly after Fulton entered the room, Doctor Quienonez returned with a pair of crutches.

"These are just in case you have too much pain when you start putting weight on that knee." He said.

"Thank you, Doctor Quienonez." Rachel said. "I only have to use them if I need them, right?" She asked.

"Only if you need them, now, that doesn't mean to favor that knee. You do need to get back to a regular routine, but in the same regard, don't overdo it, and by all means, use the crutches if you need them." He advised.

The doctor gave Rachel her discharge papers and a prescription for pain. Then, he wished her well, and he was gone.

Rachel was so excited to get back to the ship; she almost forgot to grab her crutches.

"Tiegs, you might want to be careful with those crutches when you get to the ship." Fulton said as they were leaving the hospital.

"I know how to use crutches, Fulton; unfortunately, this isn't the first time I've had to use them." Rachel said.

"No, I mean that they usually don't keep people on board who are on crutches. It's too hard to go up and down the ladders and through the hatches. It's considered a Fire Hazard." Fulton informed her.

"Yeah, but I don't necessarily need mine. I mean they're not mandatory. The doctor said so; he even put it in my orders." Rachel was getting nervous. "What if she still wound up back in the States anyway?"

"That's probably gonna be what saves you." Fulton said.

"God, I hope so." Rachel said still feeling uneasy.

Fulton and Melissa helped Rachel onto the boat that would take them all back to the USS Pennington.

The ride was only about thirty minutes long, but to Rachel it seemed like hours. She focused on the water and the sky. The temperature out on the water was a bit cooler than on land. The breeze on her face felt so good.

Rachel thought about what Melissa had said about Mitch. Sure, she wanted to see Mitch but not the way she implied. They were only friends no matter what everyone else thought.

The ship was coming into view now. Rachel was so excited she had to force herself to sit down. Fifteen minutes later they were pulling up to the barge that was anchored to the ship. Fulton helped Rachel up the bow, while Melissa carried her bags and her crutches.

Rachel thought she heard someone call her name. She looked up, shielding her eyes with her hand. On the Boat Deck standing by the railing was Hannah waving like crazy. Rachel smiled. She waved back. Then, she noticed that Hannah wasn't alone. Standing next to her were Frank and Mitch, both waving and smiling down at her. Suddenly caught off guard, Rachel got a nervous lump in her stomach. She hadn't expected to experience such feelings from seeing someone she considered "just a friend." Rachel thought again about what Melissa said at the hospital. "Could she have been right? But if she did have feelings for Mitch, wouldn't she have known it before Melissa or anyone else?" Rachel looked back at

Melissa and got the answer to the questions she'd just asked herself. Melissa had promised Rachel that she wouldn't say "I told you so." But Rachel could see that very phrase written in big bold letters all over Melissa's face. It was in the very confident smile that she flashed at Rachel.

"Oh, shut up, Melissa." Rachel told her friend.

"What did I say?" Melissa said pretending to be surprised.

"What's up with you two?" Fulton asked completely in the dark.

"I'll tell you later." Melissa told him in a whisper while laughing to herself as she walked onto the ship. "I will tell you this though; things in Deck Dept are about to get exciting, especially in third division." She said still laughing.

CHAPTER SIX

The ship seemed brand new to Rachel. It felt like she'd been gone for years. She never thought she'd miss something as cold and gray as a ship, but she actually longed for her life aboard the huge vessel.

Before she could go and see her friends, she had to check in with Medical. Then, she had to check back into Deck Dept.

She passed a few people on the way to sick call who welcomed her back. Rachel never even thought that these people knew she existed. It was starting to feel like...home.

By evening chow (dinnertime), Rachel was finished checking in. Medical had officially deemed Rachel "fit for duty" although it would be light duty. Still, she was able to stay in Cuba, and that was all that mattered to her.

Rachel was down in the berthing. She had just finished putting her clothes in her rack and had just closed it when she heard some of the ladies coming down the ladder. They were coming down to get washed and cleaned for chow. Rachel couldn't get over the fact that everyone seemed genuinely glad to see her. She was talking to one of the younger girls when she heard it.

"Rachel Tiegs. Rachel Tiegs. Where for art thou, Rachel Tiegs," the familiar voice said. Rachel started to laugh.

She turned to see Hannah standing at the bottom of the ladder.

"What's up. 'Rachel T?'" Hannah said as she ran over and gave Rachel a big hug.

"God, Hannah, I missed you so much. I couldn't wait to get back to the ship." Rachel answered.

"Yeah, I'm surprised to see you back too, but we'll discuss that later." Hannah said with a look that said, "You've got some explaining to do."

"You coming to chow with me?" She asked almost expecting Rachel to say no.

"Yeah, I'm actually looking forward to some American food. Hell, I'm looking forward to some American English." Rachel said, and they both laughed.

"Come on, I'm ready if you are." Hannah said. "The line is already long, and I'm hungry.

"I'm ready." Rachel said.

The girls headed on up the ladder to the Mess Decks. Hannah was right. The line was long. Whenever the Galley served lasagna, most of the crew would come down to eat. Rachel told Hannah about her stay at the hospital while they stood in line. After the girls got their trays, they found a seat at an empty table.

Hannah got up to go and get something to drink. She asked Rachel what she wanted to drink.

"I can get it, Hannah; you don't have to treat me like a baby." Rachel said as she began to get up.

"I know you can get it, but I want to get for you. Besides, ain't no use in both of us getting up and leaving our trays." Hannah explained.

"Now, what did you want to drink?" Hannah asked again.

"Dr. Pepper, please. Rachel said knowing there was no since in arguing, especially when Hannah was right.

"Thanks, Lil' Bits." Rachel said.

"You're welcome, not much taller." Hannah answered laughing.

Rachel was starving for some "real food," as she put it. She sat looking around the Mess Decks. She was so excited to be back. Rachel didn't notice Mitch across the room. So, he circled around the Mess Decks so that he could come up behind her and surprise her.

Hannah was on the way back with their drinks, and Rachel was focused on her. Suddenly, everything went black. Someone had placed their hands over Rachel's eyes from behind.

"Guess who, Rachel?" The deep voice asked.

Rachel knew the voice. She knew the person. What she didn't know or understand was why all of a sudden did she have a major case of butterflies. She didn't answer the person covering her eyes. She figured she'd play a game of her own. She just sat there smiling, not moving, not talking, just waiting.

"Finally," Mitch said. "Dag, Rach, you been gone that long; you don't know me?" He said almost sounding hurt, but he didn't remove his hands from her eyes.

"I knew who you were Mitch." She said deciding to let him off the hook. "I just wanted to see what you would do if I didn't say anything at all."

Mitch removed his hands and sat down next to Rachel.

"Hey Hannah." He said.

"Hey Mitch." She answered.

"So, Rachel, what in the world made you come back? I heard you had a chance to go back to V.A.

"Yeah, I did, but I figured that I might as well stay and learn whatever it is I'm supposed to learn in Cuba." She said.

For some reason though, when she explained to Mitch why she decided to stay, it all sounded like a load of bull.

"You know they got you on the watch bill already; we got the Mid-Watch together." He said.

"Damn, they don't waste no time." Hannah said.

"Well, I might as well jump back in; that's the reason I came back to the ship in the first place." Rachel said wondering if she sounded as stupid to Hannah and Mitch as she did to herself.

"Mmmm hmmm, sure that's the reason." Hannah said sarcastically.

"Well, that answered that question." Rachel thought.

Rachel cut her eyes at Hannah as if to say, "Don't start." Hannah got the message, but at the same time vowed to herself to find out exactly why Rachel did decide to stay in Cuba.

Mitch sat with the girls for a few minutes longer; then he got up to leave.

"I'll see you guys on the Boat Deck." He said as he left the table.

Rachel tried hard not to meet Hannah's eyes after Mitch left. She kept her eyes on her food, eating like she was starving, when in reality, she'd lost her appetite the moment Mitch touched her, and she realized who he was.

What in the world was wrong with her? She and Mitch were just friends. Isn't that what they kept insisting. He had a steady girlfriend back home in Ohio, not to mention a pregnant "whatever you want to call her" back in Virginia. She had to get her head on straight and think of Mitch as the friend he was and accept the fact that he would never be anything more.

"Ow," Rachel yelped, after being rudely brought out of her deep thoughts by a kick on the shin from Hannah.

"Do you want to tell me what your problem is?" Rachel asked.

"Sorry, I didn't mean to kick you that hard." Hannah apologized, but the apology didn't seem sincere to Rachel.

"You shouldn't have kicked me at all, or did you forget that you're wearing steel toe boots?" Rachel said.

"I said I'm sorry." Hannah said with an attitude.

"Yeah right, you sound real sorry." Rachel answered with an attitude of her own.

Hannah realized that she was probably not handling the situation the right way, so she softened her voice and tried again.

"Look Rach, I am sorry for real. I'm just curious about why you stayed in Cuba when you could have gone back to V.A."

Hannah said, "But." before Rachel could answer she added.

"And don't give me that bull about wanting to learn what you came here to learn. Please, this is me, and I already know why you stayed. I just want to hear it from your own mouth." Hannah said.

Rachel felt trapped. She knew she couldn't lie to Hannah, because she knew her to well. "Time to fess up." She thought.

"Okay, I'll admit I did miss Mitch while I was gone, but I missed you just as much as I missed him." She tried to justify.

"Okay, I'll give you that, but you didn't stay in Cuba for me." Hannah said.

"Okay, okay, I do think I'm starting to like Mitch as more than just a friend. But I don't even know when it happened." She said truthfully.

"Oh, that's easy." Hannah said. "While you were gone, you know what they say, 'Absence makes the heart grow fonder.'" She said with confidence.

"Yeah, but they also say, 'Out of sight, Out of mind.'" Rachel argued back.

"Well that part is true too cause your butt probably didn't give me a second thought." Hannah said jokingly.

"Yes, I did." Rachel laughed. "You know you my girl." She added.

The girls got up to take their trays up. Hannah knew that Rachel admitting that she had feelings for Mitch was only the beginning of her problems, and she didn't want her friend to get hurt. She also knew that she had to let Rachel make her own decisions even if they turned out to be the wrong ones.

"Seriously though, Rach, you know Mitch has a lot of baggage to be so young." Hannah said in a very serious voice. "Just be careful. I mean I know he's nice and everything, but that don't mean he can't hurt you." She added hoping that she wasn't overstepping her bounds as a friend.

"I know, but you are the one who said I need to get a life." Rachel reminded. "And that's all I'm trying to do. But just the same, don't worry; I'll be careful."

"Okay, I'm not gonna act like your mom, so I'll just drop it. I just care about you, and I don't want you to get hurt." Hannah said.

"I know, and I do appreciate it." Rachel said. She realized just how much Hannah cared about her, and she was grateful. Nonetheless, Mitch cared about her too. Anyway, just because she had feelings for Mitch didn't mean he felt the same way. As far as she was concerned, they were now, and would remain, just friends.

"Come on." Hannah said. "Let's get back up on deck before we're late."

"I'm so glad today is our last day in Cuba. I can't wait to get back to V.A. and go to Pizza Hut." Rachel said excited.

"Oh really, well if you wanted Pizza Hut that bad, you woulda took your butt back when you had a chance." Hannah said.

"So much for not acting like my mom." Rachel said.

"Sorry, but I couldn't resist. Besides, you left yourself wide open for that one." She said ginning.

"Anyway." Rachel said. "What time are we pulling out tomorrow?"

"Ten o'clock tomorrow morning." Hannah said. "I can't wait either." She added.

"You ready?" She asked Rachel as she stood up.

"Yeah." Rachel answered.

The girls left the Mess Decks and headed back up to the Boat Deck. Once there, they would receive their orders on what to do to get ready to get underway in the morning. Although Rachel was excited about going back to Virginia, she was equally excited about standing watch with Mitch the following night. She hoped she didn't give herself away about how she felt about him.

She didn't want to do or say anything that would hurt their friendship, unless of course Mitch wanted something more than friendship. Mitch was always so easy to talk to about anything.

Rachel wondered if she should just tell him how she felt and just deal with whatever he said.

"Nah," She thought, "I'm not that bold." But as she thought about it more a smile spread across her pretty face. "Or am I."

CHAPTER SEVEN

Rachel was standing on the Portside watching the waves. She didn't know how long she'd been standing there. After the ship had gotten underway, (two hours late) she went out there to clear her mind. She'd been thinking about Corey all day. She hadn't heard from him in over two months. As far as she was concerned, it was over, but she still couldn't move on until someone (either she or Corey) made it official.

Rachel had written him a letter late last night. She explained that she didn't feel like she was part of a couple anymore and that she felt they both should go on with their lives without each other. In reality, that's what was happening anyway. She completed the letter by telling him that she was only a phone call away and would always be there for him if he ever needed her. She placed her engagement ring inside and mailed it off that morning before the ship got underway.

She wondered if she'd done the right thing by sending a letter. She'd told Hannah that she didn't want to send a "Dear John" letter, and yet that's exactly what she'd done. She looked down at the water as the ship just cut right through it. It really did look like someone had taken a giant bottle of blue dye and poured it into the ocean. The water looked so tranquil. Rachel smiled as she spotted a few flying fish. She'd never seen anything like it before, except in the Encyclopedia.

She sucked in her breath as she saw a family of dolphins swimming next to the ship. Rachel felt like a little girl. She had to remind herself that there were other people around. She didn't want anyone to think that a few dolphins fascinated her, but in truth, she was blown away.

Rachel knew it was time to go back into the skin of the ship because her knee was starting to ache a little. She turned away from the railing and started inside. It would be time for dinner soon, but she didn't have an appetite at all. She'd actually been standing out there for over two hours. No wonder her knee was hurting. She wanted to stay and watch the sunset.

Everyone talked about how it literally took one's breath away to watch a sunrise or a sunset on the ocean. Well, she'd have to catch it another time. She wanted to go and get a few hours of sleep before her Mid Watch tonight.

"Rachel, wake up." Hannah said. But Rachel had fallen asleep with her headphones on. Hannah removed the headphones from her ears causing Rachel to jump with a start.

"I'm sorry, Boo." Hannah said apologetically. "I didn't mean to scare you, but you asked me to wake you up at 11:00 for your watch."

"It's okay. I'm still trying to get used to sleeping in this matchbox. Thanks for getting me up." She said.

"No problem." Hannah said. She wondered how her friend was doing. She'd been so quiet since they pulled out from Cuba.

"Rachel, are you okay?" Hannah asked. "You been acting funny all day."

"Oh, I'm sorry, Hannah, I didn't mean to be that way." Rachel said.

"No, not funny toward me, just funny like something's on your mind." Hannah said. "You just been more quiet than usual." She added.

"Oh, I'm all right." She lied.

Hannah got the hint that Rachel didn't want to talk so she just decided to leave her to her own thoughts.

"Okay, but if you decide you want to talk about it, you know I'm here." She said concerned. "Okay?"

"Okay." Rachel answered.

Hannah went back to her rack. Rachel went on into the head and started getting ready for her watch. After her shower, she got dressed and put her hair up. She still had twenty minutes before she had to report to the Bridge. She wondered if Hannah was still awake; she walked over to the rack. Hannah slept over in a small area where there were only two racks, and her bunkmate was on watch right now.

Rachel noticed that Hannah's curtain was closed, so she started to walk away. She didn't want to wake her.

Besides, she should have talked to her when Hannah was offering an ear.

"I'm not sleep Rachel; what's wrong? You looked so lost." Hannah said.

"You sure I'm not keeping you up?" Rachel asked.

"I'm sure. Now, spill it." Hannah said pretending to be firm.

"Okay, here's the thing," She said as she sat down on Hannah's rack. "You know I haven't heard from Corey in over two months, right?"

"Yeah," Hannah said wondering where she was going with the conversation. Hannah was expecting Rachel to say something about Mitch. "What, don't tell me you heard from him?" She said excited.

"No, but I mailed him a letter this morning." Rachel said.

"Saying what?" Hannah asked.

"I told him that I don't feel like I'm any part of a couple anymore and that I think we should both move on." She said.

"Okay, but why do you look like you want to say more?" Hannah asked suspiciously.

"I mailed his ring back to him in the letter." Rachel admitted.

"Okay, now first, I'm gonna have to get on you because you swore up and down that you wasn't gonna write him a 'Dear John' letter." Hannah said looking like the cat that had swallowed the canary. "Second and the most important point is that you finally realized that he don't deserve your dirty laundry."

Rachel laughed, but Hannah felt that there was still something that she wasn't saying.

"Okay. Are you gonna give me all of it, or are you gonna keep giving me little bits and pieces to keep me hanging on the edge of my seat?" She was getting impatient now, and she seemed to be forgetting that it was after 11:00 at night and way past Taps.

"Shhhhhh." Rachel put her finger to lips.

"Rachel, you did the right thing; what are you worried about?" Hannah asked.

"Well, what if I did it for another reason? I mean, what if there was more than one reason why I broke up with Corey?" She said.

"Oh, now, I get it, you're talking about Mitch." Hannah said suddenly seeing the whole picture.

"Sssssss, you want to say it a little louder. I don't think you woke up everybody." Rachel hissed. Hannah laughed.

"Oh, girl please, who don't know that you and Mitch got the hots for each other?" She said laughing even harder.

"We don't." Rachel insisted. "Well, at least he don't know how I feel, and I'm definitely confused about how he feels."

"What's confusing? Has he done anything or said anything to make you think that he wants to be more than friends?" Hannah asked.

"No, not really. It's just the way he looks at me sometimes or the way I feel when he looks at me." Rachel said. "I don't know what to think."

"Well baby girl, all I can tell you is follow your heart. But just remember while you're following your heart that he has a baby on the way and a girlfriend in Ohio. So, just be careful." Hannah said in a much more serious voice.

"I don't mean to throw ice water on you, Rach. I just want you to keep you wits about yourself and go slow." She added. "Okay?"

"Okay." Rachel answered. "I'll be careful."

"Good, now get your ass off my rack and go ahead up on the bridge so I can get some sleep." Hannah said laughing.

Rachel laughed too. "You so stupid. I'll see you in the morning. Thanks for listening, Hannah; I really appreciate it." Rachel said.

"I know you do, Rach. I told you I'm always here for you. Now, get out!" She said trying to hide her laughter.

"I'm gone." Rachel said laughing as she got up and left. She went back to her rack and got her cover (hat), her jacket, and a pen, and off she went to the bridge.

CHAPTER EIGHT

Rachel stepped onto the Bridge and into total darkness. She stood still for a couple of minutes to let her eyes adjust. When she could see where she was going, she walked across the Bridge and out onto the Portside.

Mitch was out there alone with his back to her. He was looking through the binoculars at another ship's light far out on the horizon.

"What's up, Tiegs?" He said without even turning around.

"How did you know it was me?" Rachel asked dumbfounded.

"I'd know your perfume anywhere. Everybody in deck knows your perfume." He answered with a smile that she couldn't' see.

"Oh, well, I hope that's a good thing." She said not sure how to react.

"That's a very good thing." Mitch said turning around flashing that beautiful smile at her.

Rachel thought her knees would buckle. He looked so good. His shirt was ironed to perfection as were his dungarees. His boots were shinning even in the dark and whatever cologne he was wearing was making her drool. "Thank God they were in the dark!" She thought.

Mitch grabbed the radio, called inside to the Bridge, and reported the ship at which he was looking. He gave the exact location of the ship in reference to the USS Pennington. His voice sounded so confident. Rachel had to make herself concentrate on standing her watch and not watching Mitch.

"How's your knee, Rachel?" He asked to make small talk. For some reason Mitch was feeling a bit nervous around her, and he hoped it wasn't showing.

"It's a lot better; it was hurting a little earlier." She said. "I think I might have been on it a bit too long today."

"Yeah, probably when you were out on the Portside earlier." He said.

"How you know I was out on Portside today; where were you?" She asked surprised.

"I was on the same side, but I was further back, near the fantail." He said.

"You should have come over and said something. I was out here all by myself." She said.

"I know; that's why I didn't. You seemed to be pretty deep in thought." He said.

"Yeah, I was. She admitted.

"Until you saw those dolphins swim by." He said laughing. "You should have seen your face. You looked like a little girl who had just saw Santa Clause."

"Oh, be quiet." She said laughing with him.

"So, what were you doing out on the fantail? Were you by yourself too, or was you with the rest of the deck dogs?" She asked jokingly.

"Nah, I was by myself, and I was doing the same thing it looked like you were doing."

"What, looking at the dolphins and the flying fish?" She asked playing surprised.

"Yeah, right." He said with a smirk.

"No, for real, I just had a lot on my mind." He said in a more serious voice.

"Okay, I'll tell you what. You tell me what's on your mind. I'll tell you what's on my mind, and in the end, maybe we can help each other." Rachel said.

"Okay, you first." Mitch said quickly.

"No, I said you tell me first." Rachel argued.

Suddenly, the Starboard Watch called on the radio to ask if Portside and Aft Watch were going to rotate with them, or if they were all going to just stay where they were.

"Hold on a second man." Mitch said. He looked at Rachel.

"You want to rotate or stay here?"

"We would be going back Aft, right?" She asked.

"Yeah." Mitch said. "We don't have to if you don't want to." He added, but inside he hoped she would want to rotate back Aft. He would love to go back Aft. It was very private back there. No one would be back there, but the two of them. They'd be able to talk without any interruptions.

"Yeah, I'd rather go back Aft. We can talk better back there. Plus, ain't no Officers to worry about back there." Rachel said as she were if reading Mitch's mind.

"Starboard, this is Port. We are gonna rotate; repeat, we are gonna rotate, over." Mitch said into the radio.

"Port, this is Aft. One of you guys come back here and relieve us, so we can relieve Starboard. Then, Starboard will relieve the other one of you to go back Aft. Over."

"Roger that Aft. Tiegs is on her way back now, over." Mitch said back.

"Roger that Port." Then, the radio was quiet.

Mitch looked at Rachel. "You gonna be all right back there til I get there?" He asked suddenly concerned that she might be afraid back there in the dark alone.

"Yeah Mitch, I'm not a little girl. I'll be fine." She said smiling.

"Yeah, I know you're fine, but that's not what I asked you." Mitch joked.

"Whatever! I'll see you in a few minutes, and you better be ready to fess up about what's on your mind." Rachel said.

"All right but be careful; it's dark back there. You are kinda accident prone, and I ain't trying to hear no 'Man overboard!'" He said laughing.

"Ha ha." Rachel said as she left the Portside.

Rachel decided to walk through the skin of the ship (inside) instead of outside. It was very dark outside, and it would be too easy to trip over a cleat in the deck and fall. She could hurt herself really easy out there in the dark, and she wasn't taking any chances with her knee.

The only problem with that decision, as she found out when she got to the fantail, was now she had to let her eyes adjust to the dark all over again.

Rachel's eyes were still adjusting to the blackness on the fantail when Mitch got back there.

"Rachel, where you at?' Mitch called out to her over the sound of the waves.

"Dag Mitch, I ain't that dark." She teased.

"Yeah, I know. As a matter of fact, if you wasn't so yellow, I wouldn't be able to see nothin'." He teased back.

"You got your nerve! At least I got black people's eyes, white boy!" She laughed.

"Yeah, but you yellow like a Rican. Mitch said laughing.

"Whatever!" Rachel conceded.

"Yeah, that's what I thought." Mitch said smiling knowing he'd won this battle.

Mitch sat down on a huge cleat next to Rachel. She had the headphones on and the radio in her hand.

"You want me to take that, or are you all right?" He asked pointing to the headphones and the radio.

"Nah, I'm good." She said nervously. All of a sudden, she was glad she had the headphones on and the radio in her hand. She would have welcomed anything that could distract her from realizing just how close they were sitting.

"All right, now you first." Rachel said. She needed to put her mind on something other than his lips. She wondered how it would feel to kiss him. She wondered if he was a good kisser. Rachel heard her name and realized that Mitch was trying to get her attention.

"I'm sorry, Mitch; what did you say?" Rachel said embarrassed. She was glad he couldn't see how red her face was. "They were saying something on the headphones, and I thought they were talking to me."

"Good save." She thought.

"I was saying that I got a letter from Melissa today." He said.

"Well, what did she say?" Rachel asked not really wanting to know but needing to find out.

"Not much." He said. "That's what's bothering me."

"What do you mean?" Rachel asked confused.

"Well, you know I gave her the money for an abortion before I left for Cuba." He said.

"Yeah." Rachel said. "Is she all right?" Rachel was concerned by the seriousness in his voice.

"Oh, yeah, she's fine." He said. "It's just that she didn't mention the baby, the abortion, or if she had enough money." He sounded confused himself. "She just kept going on and on about how much she loves me and misses me. She keeps talking about us working things out."

"Okay, I think I see the problem now." Rachel said.

"I mean I've told Melissa over and over again that we don't go together, and we don't have anything to work out." He said. He was starting to get upset now. "Sometimes she acts like she's in another world or something, like fatal attraction."

Rachel started to laugh so hard that Mitch couldn't help but start laughing along with her.

"It ain't funny Rachel," Mitch said still laughing.

"I know it ain't, but you just sounded so childlike. You were actually whining." She said.

"Hey, I don't whine." He said trying to keep a straight face.

"Trust me. You sounded like Dennis the Menace." Rachel joked.

"Oh, you got jokes right?" Mitch said smiling.

"Hey, I made you laugh, and it got your mind off your problems for a minute." She added.

"All right, how 'bout we change the subject? Why don't you tell me what's was bothering you today when I saw you talking to the dolphins." Mitch said barely able to keep from bursting into laughter.

"You're not funny." Rachel said trying hard not to laugh. She could only imagine what she must have looked like today, grinning like a fool at a bunch of dolphins.

Finally, after giving it some thought, she told Mitch what was bothering her.

"Okay, you remember my fiancé, Corey, right?" She asked.

"Yeah, the one you haven't heard from in almost three months. What about him?" Mitch said with more attitude that he intended.

Rachel hesitated for a second. "Was that irritation in Mitch's voice that she heard?" She thought to herself. "But why would he have a problem with Corey? He'd never even met him." Rachel dismissed it and went on telling Mitch her problem.

"Well, this morning before the ship got underway, I mailed Corey a 'Dear John' letter. I told him that I didn't feel like I'm a part of a couple anymore. I feel like we've drifted apart and that we should move on."

"Well, I still have yet to see the problem." Mitch said. Somehow Rachel's news that she'd broken up with Corey made his heart light. It almost made him forget about his own problems.

"Well," Rachel continued, "I also sent his ring back to him in this letter." She said. She almost felt ashamed about the way she'd handled things. She wondered what Mitch would think of her. She also wondered why she even cared what he thought at all.

"Aw, that's cold." He said, but he was laughing.

"What's so funny?" Rachel asked surprised at his sudden outburst of laughter.

"I didn't think you could do something cold like that." He said. "You don't come off to me like the vindictive type."

"Mitch!" Rachel said raising her voice in surprise. "I wasn't trying to be vindictive. I just didn't want Corey to think I was trying to keep his ring." Rachel said. "Oh my God." She thought out loud. "What if he thinks I was trying to be smart?"

Mitch saw that Rachel was actually getting upset at the thought that someone she cared about might be mad at her. Especially when she was only trying to do what she thought was the right thing.

"Look here." He said. "Did you write anything in your letter that might lead Corey to believe that you were trying to be smart?" He asked suddenly feeling a strong need to ease her mind.

"No, nothing at all." Rachel said defensively. "As a matter of fact, I told him that I'd always be here for him and that I was only a phone call away if he ever needed me." She added.

For some reason, knowing that Rachel had pledged her friendship to someone who treated her like she didn't matter made Mitch mad all over again. However, this time he was more worried about making Rachel feel better, not himself. Actually, the thought of making her feel better made him smile inside.

"Well then." He said. "If this Corey knows you at all, he'll know that you weren't trying to be smart. You say you two were close, right?"

"Yeah, very close." Rachel said.

"Then, don't worry." He said. "Besides, he's gotta know that not calling or writing for almost three months wasn't a good thing as far as relationships go. You did do anything wrong Rach. He did."

"You really think so?" She said hopefully.

"I know so." He said.

Mitch gazed into Rachel's eyes. She had the deepest, most beautiful dark brown eyes he'd ever seen. He loved her eyes and her lips. He wanted so badly to hold her and to kiss her. Was he mistaken, or was he seeing the same longing in her eyes? "Well." He thought. "There was only one way to find out." He knew that it was almost 3:15 am, and they only had 30 minutes left on watch. Because of the late hour, no one was around. So, he decided to just do it.

Rachel was lost in those hazel eyes. She had seen very clearly the longing and desire in his eyes. She'd never had anyone look at her that way before. She wanted so badly to open up and tell him that she no longer thought of him as a friend and that she was so attracted to him that she could barely direct her thoughts anywhere else. She was hoping he would tell her that he felt the same way, but how could he feel the same way? He had two other women who were probably taking up all the space in his heart that was available.

"Rachel." Mitch said softly.

"Hmmmm." It was the only response she could muster up after staring into his beautiful eyes.

"Would you get mad if I kissed you?"

"There…" He'd said it. "Now what?" He thought.

"Actually Mitch, I'd be upset if you didn't." She said barely above a whisper.

Rachel could hear her heart beating in her ears. Mitch placed his finger under her chin and tilted her face up towards his. He placed a kiss so softly upon her lips that she almost wondered if it really happened. Still with his lips slightly against hers, he whispered. "I've been wanting to do this for so long, but I didn't want to risk losing you as a friend."

"Sorry to break it to you, Mitch, but from the moment you kissed me, we no longer had a friendship." Rachel teased.

"We have something, but I wouldn't call it a friendship. I don't usually kiss my friends like that." She said smiling.

"I guess we got some things to talk about, huh?" He said.

"You think?" Rachel said laughing nervously.

"Rachel, I know you just broke up with your fiancé, and I'm not trying to horde in on someone else's territory, but I couldn't hold my feelings back for another minute." He confessed.

"I don't think I could have taken much more of this 'we're just friends' mess anymore myself." Both laughed.

"You know everybody's gonna think we were lying along." Mitch said.

"I don't care; do you?" Rachel said.

Mitch leaned over and kissed Rachel so deeply that she was sure her toes curled up. "God." She thought. "But he was a great kisser."

Finally, Mitch pulled away reluctantly. "Does that answer your question?" He said.

"Definitely." She answered.

"We better chill out." Mitch said although chilling out was the last thing he wanted. He could go on kissing Rachel all night. Nevertheless, if the wrong person caught them, they could both wind up in front of the captain. Moreover, Mitch didn't want to do anything to place Rachel in jeopardy.

"Yeah, we better get ready to turn over the watch." She said.

"Will I see you tomorrow?" He said.

"Of course, we have some talking to do, remember?" She said smiling.

"Yeah, we definitely have some things to discuss." He agreed.

Before they knew it, Mitch and Rachel were relieved from watch. Rachel hated to leave. She knew that she wouldn't get any sleep tonight. Mitch walked her to her berthing. He wanted so badly to kiss her goodbye, but they both knew that was out of the question because they were inside of the ship. Not to mention Rachel's berthing was right next to the Master at Arms Office (the ship's police). They said goodbye at the top of the ladder that led to her berthing. Mitch walked on further to his own berthing wondering also if he'd be able to sleep tonight and knowing for a fact that he wouldn't be.

CHAPTER NINE

"Moored, shift colors," Sounded out over the intercom. The ship was finally back in Virginia at Pier 21. It seemed like years since the USS Pennington had been there. Rachel couldn't wait to step foot on dry "American" land again.

She and Mitch had grown so very close. They were already close before, but now their relationship had taken a drastic turn. As much as she cared for Mitch, she still wasn't sure if the turn their relationship had taken was for the better. They both were coming into this relationship with major baggage. Even so, Rachel knew that she was always the kind of woman who followed her heart, and this time would be no different. She felt that as close as she and Mitch were, they could weather any storm.

The Deck Dept was just putting the bow down and making sure it was secured. Rachel looked up at the crane. Mitch was operating. Her heart swelled so with pride; she was afraid that it would explode. She loved to watch him work. He looked down where she was and winked at her. "Oh God." She thought. "If he only knew what just that little gesture did to her, he would stop." She smiled back.

Mitch and Rachel had made plans to meet at "Tradewinds," the club on base. Rachel had only been there twice, but she liked the atmosphere a lot. She was supposed to meet Mitch there around ten.

She was so excited. She actually had to calm herself down. She was also very nervous. She had no idea what the evening would bring. It was so different on the ship, because no matter how many times she and Mitch stole kisses, she knew that it wouldn't go any further because of where they were. Now that they were back in Virginia, when things got heated, would she be able to stop? Would she even want to?

Rachel got a lump in her stomach just imagining being intimate with Mitch. She wondered what kind of lover he was. He was four years younger than she was. The funny part was, although she wasn't a virgin, she really wasn't very experienced where men were concerned.

Somehow, she figured Mitch was more experienced than she was. She hoped she wouldn't be a disappointment to him. "Rachel, get a grip." She said quietly to herself. "You don't even know if things will go that far." She scolded herself. "Don't rush it; just let things happen."

"Tiegs." Rachel was brought out of her thoughts. She turned to see Londa Wilkens walking toward her with Hannah.

"What's up Hannah, Londa." Rachel said.

"What you doing when you get off the ship?" Londa asked.

Londa was about 5'3" and very thin. She probably weighed about 115 lbs, but she had a very nice figure. Nevertheless, for a black girl, she needed more butt. Londa wasn't exactly what you would call cute. As a matter of fact, she was what Rachel's mom would call "Monkey Cute." She was kind of in between cute and ugly. She had a sailor vocabulary, and she would cuss you out in a New York minute. Londa was from Tulsa Ok. She and Rachel became friends when she found out that

Rachel's mom was from Lawton Ok. Rachel was always grateful that Londa was her friend and not her enemy.

"I'm meeting Mitch at Tradewinds." Rachel answered, noticing the look that Hannah and Londa exchanged.

"What?" She replied preparing herself what she knew was about to come.

"I knew ya'll was more than just some friends." Londa accused laughing.

"No, we wasn't; we just starting when I got back to the ship in Cuba." Rachel insisted. "Tell her Hannah."

"It's true; they only been talking for a few weeks. But I think they liked each other all along, they just didn't know it." She added.

"Don't get me wrong, Rachel." Londa said still smiling. "I'm glad ya'll finally hooked up. Mitch is cool, and ya'll make a nice couple. But don't he got a girlfriend back at home in Ohio?" She asked.

"We haven't really talked about Becca yet." Rachel admitted. "But we know we got a lot to talk about."

"Becca? She white ain't she?" Londa asked. "Mitch know he like hisself some white girls."

"True." Hannah agreed laughing.

"Well anyway, that ain't even none of my business." Londa said.

"True again." Hannah said still laughing.

"Oh, be quiet Hannah." Londa said laughing also.

"We just wanted to know if you wanted to catch a cab to the club with us, and we can just hang out together until you hook up with Mitch." Londa said.

"Yeah, that's cool with me because I really don't want to walk in by myself." Rachel said. "What time are you guys leaving?"

"Probably around nine." Hannah said. "Is that all right with everybody?"

"Fine with me." Rachel said

"Me too." Londa agreed.

"You guys eating on the ship?" Rachel asked.

"I'm not." Hannah answered.

"Why? You want to leave a little earlier and go get something to eat?' Londa asked.

"Do you guys mind? It don't have to be anything special. We can walk over to Burger King. I'm just tired of Galley food." Rachel said.

"No problem, say about seven-thirty?" Londa said.

"That's good." Hannah said.

"That's perfect." Rachel agreed.

Fulton walked over to where the girls were standing.

"You guys want to do me a favor and get everybody started on sweepers. That way when we get done securing everything, we can knock off. We can probably be outta here by 1300." He said.

"Hey 1300 sounds good to us." Londa said wih excitement.

"I know that's right." Hannah said. "I might even be able to get me a nap; shoot, I had the four to eight this morning. I am so sleepy." She added.

Rachel was so in another world she barely knew what was going on around her. All she could think about was seeing Mitch in some other setting than the USS Pennington. Still, as much as she wanted to be alone with him, she was also just that much more nervous about being alone with him.

CHAPTER TEN

Rachel, Hannah, and Londa all shared a cab to Tradewinds. It was only a short ten-minute ride from Pier 21 to the club. Rachel was so nervous; she couldn't eat more than a handful of French fries when they went to Burger King.

Hannah and Londa both got on her about not eating. They said, "If you plan to drink anything, you're gonna need something in your stomach."

Rachel knew they were right. But the last thing on her mind was her stomach, except maybe the large lump that was laying in the bottom of it.

The cab pulled up in front of the club. It was only 9:30, so it wasn't packed. Nevertheless, there was still a pretty big line forming outside. The girls got in the line and were at the door before they knew it. They showed their I. D.'s, paid the cover charge, and went inside. By this time, it was 9:45. Rachel was so nervous; she was having a hard time keeping down the few fries she managed to eat.

"I have to go to the bathroom." Hannah said. "Rach, come go with me."

"Okay, I gotta go anyway." Rachel said.

"I'll see y'all inside; I need a drink." Londa said. "I'll see if I can find a table."

"All right." Hannah said.

The girls went on into the bathroom. They were both shocked to see that there was no line. Rachel went into the first empty stall she saw. Hannah stopped in front of the mirror first to check her make-up. It didn't escape her how nervous Rachel was.

"You okay, Rach?" She asked out loud because they were the only two in the room.

"Yeah, I'll be fine." She said as she came out of the stall. She washed her hands and looked around for a paper towel.

"I'm just a little nervous. Maybe I'll feel more relaxed when I get me a drink." She added.

"I know I can't wait to get me one, or two, or three. All I know is that I better not have to pay for any of them." Hannah said jokingly.

Rachel checked her hair and make-up in the mirror. She wanted to look perfect for Mitch. She had on a tight looking, but not fitting pair of straight legged jeans, and a navy-blue cardigan with a white T-Shirt underneath. That seemed to be the style in Norfolk. Her hair was curled and swept up into a banana clip, but it was still long enough to touch the nape of her neck.

Hannah and Rachel circled the club one full time. They finally spotted Londa on the second round. She was sitting at a booth with a few other people from the ship. Londa waved them over.

The music in the club was a large mixture of Rock, R&B, slow, and Country. Rachel liked pretty much all music, but she really didn't care for Hard Rock. That was Hannah's thing.

The girls sat down, and a few minutes later, a barmaid came over and took their drink order. Hannah ordered a Long Island Iced Tea, as did the rest of the table. Rachel ordered a Rum and Coke.

"You oddball." Londa said laughing.

"I can't drink real sweet drinks." Rachel said laughing along with everyone else.

"Why not?" Hannah asked genuinely curious.

"Because, if they taste too good, I'll forget that there's liquor in them, and y'all will be picking me up off the floor." She explained.

"Besides," she added "I want to keep my wits about myself tonight. I don't want anything happening strictly because 'I was drunk.' Know what I mean?"

"That makes since." Hannah agreed.

The barmaid returned with the drinks. Everyone paid for their own individual drink and gave their own individual tips.

"Man, they don't never bring your drink that fast." Londa said. "She just know today was our payday. That hussy was working for them tips."

"Long as it taste good, who cares?" Hannah said taking a long drag from her straw.

"What does that taste like, Hannah?" Rachel asked.

"It's good; it taste just like Iced Tea." Hannah answered. "Here taste it." She passed her glass to Rachel. Rachel took a sip. She rolled the liquid around on her tongue and swallowed.

"Ain't it good?" Hannah asked excitedly.

"It's all right, but it's a little to tart for me." Rachel said trying not to offend anyone, since they all had the same drink.

"I thought you didn't like sweet drinks." Londa said confused. You should like it if it's tart.

"I don't like sweet drinks, but that don't mean I want to drink something that taste like a lemon either." Rachel argued back.

"Whatever." Londa said with a slight attitude. "Drink what you like."

"That's exactly what I'm doing." Rachel said, and don't be getting mad at me cause I don't like your drink, Londa, Londa." Rachel teased.

"Oh, shut up, Rachel." Londa said laughing.

"Ooh, that's my song." Hannah said. "I gotta go get my dance on." She got up and started to scoot out of the booth.

Rachel and Londa noticed that the song was some Rock and Roll number. They looked at each other with a frown. Then, with the same look glued to their faces, they both looked at Hannah.

"Oh forget y'all." She said to both of them laughing. She asked them to watch her drink, and she headed for the dance floor.

Rachel and Londa sat there laughing for a few minutes.

"And you cracked on me about what I do and don't drink." Rachel said between laughter.

"I know right." Londa said laughing so hard; she thought she'd wet herself.

"I gotta go to the bathroom." She said still laughing. "You gonna be all right?"

"Yeah, I'm good; go ahead." Rachel said.

Rachel was feeling much more relaxed now. She'd almost finished her first drink. As the barmaid passed her table, Rachel ordered another Rum and Coke. When the barmaid returned with her order, Rachel pulled out her money to pay for her drink.

"I got this." Mitch said from behind. He paid the barmaid for Rachel's drink and ordered one for himself.

"How long you been here?" Rachel asked smiling more than she meant to, but she couldn't help it. She was so glad to see him.

"Not long, about twenty minutes, just long enough to circle once around. I'm surprised I found you on the first round. It's packed in here."

"Yeah, and it just got this full over the past half hour." Rachel said.

"Who you here with? I know all these drinks ain't yours." Mitch said jokingly.

"Yeah right." Rachel said. "No, Hannah went to go dance, and Londa's in the bathroom."

"Hannah went to dance? To this?" He said with the same frown on his face that she and Londa had worn. Rachel couldn't help but laugh.

"I know," she said "That's why Londa went to the bathroom; she almost peed herself laughing.

"Oh, thanks for the drink." She said when she realized that she never said thank you.

"You're very welcome." He said smiling the most beautiful smile. "Are you nervous being with me, Rachel?" Mitch asked when he noticed her blushing.

"A little." She admitted. "I don't know why with as much time as we spend together."

"It's okay, I won't bite. Besides I'm a little nervous myself. But I couldn't wait to see you. You look very nice."

"Thank you." She said blushing even more. "So, do you." Mitch was wearing a pair of black jeans and a nice shirt. But it was his cologne that was driving her crazy.

Hannah returned to the table a few minutes later. She noticed that Londa was now gone, and Mitch had joined them. She also noticed how he and Rachel were looking at each other. She thought they made a nice couple.

"Hey Mitch." She said as she approached the table.

"What's up, Hannah?" He said. "Hope you don't mind me joining y'all.

"Not at all, we all family!" She said laughing.

Mitch and Rachel both laughed too. The three of them sat and talked for over an hour. Londa came back long enough to retrieve her drink, and let the girls know that she and "a friend" were leaving. She told them that she would see them later, and she left.

Rachel was feeling warm and relaxed after she finished her second drink. Soon the club lights went down, and a slow song came on. Mitch asked Rachel if she wanted to dance, and she said yes.

Mitch took Rachel by the hand and led her through the crowded room to the dance floor. When he put his arms around her waist, she thought she would melt. They danced to "Make It Last Forever" by Keith Sweat, and that was exactly how Rachel felt. She wanted the dance to last forever. She never wanted to leave the warmth and security of Mitch's arms.

Rachel didn't know if she was "buzzing" from the Rum and Coke or the heady scent of his cologne. She laid her head on his shoulder, and he held her even closer. Rachel kissed Mitch lightly on his neck. "God, he smelled so good." She said to herself.

Mitch looked down into Rachel's eyes and got lost in the depth of their darkness. He leaned down and kissed her. Her lips were so soft and delicious. Finally, Mitch ended the kiss reluctantly. Rachel looked up at him shyly with desire evident in her eyes.

"You want to go somewhere else?" He asked hoping she said yes, but afraid she wouldn't. He wanted her so badly, but he didn't want to scare her away.

"Where?" Rachel asked. She felt like she was under some spell. She wanted to be with Mitch. She wanted to make love to him. However, what if she did, and their relationship changed in a way that neither of them liked?

Sensing her hesitation, Mitch wanted to ease her mind.

"Look Rachel, I'm not gonna lie to you. I do want you, bad. But if you're not ready, I can wait. Even if you never want to take this any further, it won't change how I feel about you."

"I trust you Mitch. Where do you want to go?" Rachel asked with her heart in her throat. She knew she should probably take it a bit slower, but she felt that she had nothing to fear from Mitch.

"You want to go get a room?" He said. Finally, he had gotten it out of his mouth. "What would she think of him?" He didn't want to move too fast, but at the same time, he felt he had to make his feelings known.

"I know you probably won't believe this, but I'd be happy just holding you in my arms all night." He said. He couldn't believe how sappy he sounded even to himself. The funny part was, it was true.

"I would love to spend the night in your arms." She was surprised to hear herself saying. "And we'll just let whatever happens...happen."

After they finished dancing, Rachel and Mitch walked over to their table. Hannah was still sitting there talking to the guy she'd been dancing with earlier. Rachel told Hannah that she and Mitch were leaving. Hannah gave her a knowing smile and said goodbye to both of them. She silently hoped that Rachel wasn't moving too fast, but at the same time, she certainly couldn't blame her.

Mitch and Rachel took a cab to the same Econo-Lodge that Rachel had stayed in before they left for Cuba. Mitch registered the room in his name. Rachel watched while he filled out the information on the card.

The hotel clerk gave Mitch a key and told him his room was on the second floor facing the street.

Once they got in the room, Rachel felt her nervousness returning. She grabbed the remote for the T.V. and turned it on. Rachel sat down on the bed, and Mitch sat down beside her. They watched T.V. for a while. Mitch looked at Rachel as she watched T.V. She was so beautiful and sexy to him. He leaned over and placed a soft gentle kiss on her neck. She turned to face him. His eyes were glazed with desire.

Mitch kissed Rachel with a kiss so deep that she felt like her body would explode from the passion she felt inside. She slipped her arms around his neck as the kiss deepened. Still, as passionate and consuming as the kiss was, the way he held her as he put his arms around her waist was gentle. She could feel how much he cared for her just by the way he held her in his arms. Their bodies were pressed together so tightly; Rachel was afraid that he could feel her heart beating wildly in her chest.

Slowly Mitch pulled away while still holding Rachel. He looked into her eyes and saw the same desire that he knew was mirrored in his own. However, he couldn't go any further until he knew that she wanted him as much as and for the same reason that he wanted her. He didn't want anything to happen because defenses were down due to alcohol.

"Rach." He said in a raspy voice that was thick with wanting. "Are you sure you want to keep this up? I don't want you to feel pressured in any way. But at the same time, I so want you so bad it hurts."

Rachel looked at Mitch through glazed eyes. Her lips were slightly swollen from being kissed so thoroughly.

"Mitch, I'm a big girl, and I know exactly what I'm doing." She said as she placed her hand gently upon his cheek.

"I want to be with you. I want you to make love to me, but I don't want to be thought of in the same way you think of Melissa. I also don't want to be thought of as just your friend." She added.

"Now, if you can't promise me more than friendship, that's fine. Just be honest with me. Okay?"

"I so want more than friendship. I want you to be mine." He said.

"Then, it looks like were on the same page." She said. "So, with that being said, will you do something for me?" She asked with a sly smile.

"Sure, anything." He said anxiously.

"Will you make love to me...now." She said.

"Say no more." He said.

Mitch stood up. He removed his shirt without ever taking his eyes off her. His skin was a beautiful bronze, and as smooth as caramel. His chest was cut, muscular, and void of any hair.

Next, he removed his pants to reveal strong muscular legs. Rachel had admired those sexy bowlegs many times, but she'd never in a million years thought that his body was so magnificent. She could feel her mouth watering.

Mitch laid back down on the bed next to Rachel, only in his underwear. He showered her lips and face with feather light kisses. He slowly removed her sweater, t-shirt, and jeans. She laid on her back looking up at him in a sexy light blue lace bra and panty set. She looked like and angel. He didn't know how much more he could take.

Rachel felt her skin burn beneath his gaze. He seemed to be in a trance as he took in every inch of her body with his eyes. He slowly ran his hands over her body. It was taking all the strength he could muster up just to take it slow, but Mitch was determined to fight off the urgency of his own needs.

Mitch wanted their first intimate journey together to be special. Her kisses were so sweet; he could feel himself slipping fast into emotions that he'd only read about. Rachel moaned lightly as their kisses grew more passionate.

Finally, when they both had removed the last barrier of clothing, they came together as one. Rachel had never experienced such wild abandonment. She'd never known such passion. Mitch whispered her name over and over again. Their union was so much more than Rachel had anticipated. Mitch held her close in his arms. He didn't want to ever let her go and vowed silently to himself that he never would.

CHAPTER ELEVEN

The days had begun to grow cooler, especially in the evenings. It was now mid-October. Rachel stood on the balcony of the same hotel she'd frequented so many times before. It was early Friday evening. Mitch was still on the ship because he had duty. He would be there the next morning as soon as his duty section turned over to the next duty section.

Rachel couldn't wait. She missed him terribly when he wasn't around. She really had to force herself to function when Mitch wasn't with her. She loved him so deeply, and she knew he felt the same way about her, maybe even more. He was so jealous of her, and she was so flattered. No man had ever cared so much about where she went, what she wore, and who she knew. They had been together for almost three months. The only thing that bothered Rachel was when Mitch got really quiet. She automatically knew what he was thinking about, Melissa, but not because he still cared about her. It was quite the opposite. He hated her. He still cursed the very day he met her.

Mitch thought he could trust Melissa. Why else would he give her almost three hundred dollars to get an abortion and not stay around to make sure she did just that?

But Melissa didn't get an abortion. When the ship pulled back in to Norfolk from Cuba, she was standing on the pier still very much in love with Mitch and still very pregnant. She had already started to show.

Mitch was so mad he probably could have killed her with his bare hands. At first, he was just pissed off that she'd spent his money and lied to him about getting an abortion she'd never planned to get. Then, it finally hit him that soon he would have a child whom he would be required to help raise, a child whom he didn't even want. Mitch had a very hard time explaining it all to Rachel. He told her about it when they spent their first night together. That was why he was so late getting to the club. He still hadn't told his parents yet, not to mention Becca. Mitch was like the golden boy of Elyria, Ohio. To tell his mom that he'd gotten some girl whom he didn't even care about, pregnant, was almost too much to bear. He knew that the news would disappoint his family deeply.

Rachel sighed as she turned to walk back into her hotel room. She was so bored. She actually felt less than alive when Mitch wasn't around. She couldn't even remember what she normally did before he came into her life.

Rachel picked up the phone and dialed the eleven numbers to call her sister, Gloria, in New Jersey. Today was October 22, Gloria's birthday. By now, she was probably getting ready to go out and celebrate her twenty-sixth birthday and was probably wondering why she had gotten a phone call from everyone except Rachel.

"Hello," Gloria answered the phone sounding out of breath.

"Happy Birthday, Gloria." Rachel said making herself sound happier than she really was.

"Hey Rachel. I was wondering if I was gonna hear from you today." She said.

"You probably thought I forgot, didn't you?" Rachael said.

"I was beginning to wonder because you never forget my birthday. When you commin home?"

"I don't know, probably in February. Why, what's going on?" Rachel asked.

"February! Why can't you come for Thanksgiving or Christmas?" Gloria asked.

Rachel could tell where this conversation was, and she knew that it wouldn't be the last time she would have this same conversation with someone in her family.

"Because I'm not; now, can we change the subject?" Rachel said, her patience now growing thin. She hated to be so short with Gloria, especially on her birthday. Gloria and Rachel had always been very close. That's why Gloria didn't hesitate to speak the truth to Rachel.

Rachel having an attitude wasn't going to change that. Gloria was the one sister out of the four who would get an attitude at the drop of a dime, and Rachel was the one sister out of the four who wouldn't hesitate to tell Gloria just where to get off, and just where she could go. Nevertheless, after all was said and done, they'd still be close.

"Don't nobody care about you getting mad, Rachel; shoot, it's my birthday. Can't nobody make me mad today, so there!" She said laughing.

"Whatever, Gloria." Rachel said laughing with her.

"No, seriously though, I was just asking cause Ra'Shaun misses you so much." Gloria confessed.

"I know; I miss my baby too." Rachel admitted. "But I just can't be in Salem around the holidays, Gloria. I just can't." Rachel said quietly.

"Okay, okay Rach, I'll leave you alone about it...for now." Gloria said.

She felt sorry for her baby sister. She could hear the fear in Rachel's voice at just the thought of being in Salem around Christmas.

"If you change your mind, let me know. Maybe you could surprise Mom. She would be so happy." Gloria said, not willing to let it go yet.

"It's not gonna happen, Gloria, at least not this year. I'll let you go now cause I'm sure you're getting ready to go out." Rachel said trying to sound lighthearted.

"You know that I'm waiting for Carol to come over now. You know we gotta have a few drinks before we leave." She said.

"Have fun, wish I could go with you." Rachel said before she thought.

"Yeah, I wish you were here too." Gloria said sarcastically.

"See you soon, Gloria. Have a Happy Birthday." Rachel said sounding sad again.

"I love you, Rachel." Gloria said.

"I love you too, Gloria. Bye." Rachel said.

"Bye." Gloria answered.

Rachel hung up the phone. She really did want to go home and see her son, Ra'Shaun, but the thought of being in Salem during the holidays scared her beyond reason.

She loved being home in Salem with her family, especially her little boy. She actually loved Salem, at any time except Christmas. It hurt to think of how she used to love the holiday season as a little girl. Now, how she wanted nothing to do with it. She hated the season of Christmas so much that it seemed to rule her very soul. She couldn't even stand to hear Christmas songs on the radio or watch Christmas specials on T.V.

Rachel could feel her hatred rising to the boiling point. She tried to put the thought of the holidays out of her head, but she couldn't erase the memory of her little boy from her mind. She missed him so very much. He was her whole world. She felt so guilty because she couldn't put her own feelings aside and put Ra'Shaun's emotional welfare ahead of her own. She wanted to, but she just didn't know how.

Finally bored to the point of actually being sleepy, Rachel took a long, hot shower and climbed into bed. She lay in bed and thought about her sister, Gloria, and what she'd said. She hadn't been home in months.

"Maybe I will go home for Thanksgiving." She said to herself. She remembered holidays from years before.

They were always such happy times. The house would be filled with family, friends, and more love than she ever thought possible.

"Yeah." She thought as she drifted off to sleep. "Maybe I will go home for Thanksgiving.

CHAPTER TWELVE

Rachel was in a deep sleep. She tried hard to awaken, but she couldn't. She knew where she was headed in this particular dream, and she didn't want to go there again. She'd been there so many times, and each time was just as vivid as the time before and just horrifying.

It seemed that the more she tried to wake up the more the dream took over. Then, as usual, she was suddenly back in her first apartment in Salem, New Jersey. It was she and her baby, Ra'Shaun. He was going to be two-years-old in just three weeks.

It was Christmas night 1985. Rachel had spent the whole day at her parents' new home, a block down the street from her own apartment. Rachel had taken over the apartment after her parents had moved out just five months earlier. She, her sister, Gloria, and some friends had planned to go out that night, but Rachel couldn't find a babysitter. So, finally around 9:30, she and Ra'Shaun walk the short block to their apartment. Ra'Shaun was so tired. This had been his second Christmas, and he'd really enjoyed himself. He was the baby of the entire family, and he was very spoiled. Nevertheless, he was also a very happy baby.

Rachel unlocked the door to her apartment and went in. She was thankful that, for once, she hadn't locked her keys inside. She went straight to Ra'Shaun's bedroom and laid him in his crib. He'd fallen asleep on her shoulder during the short walk home. She covered him up and left his room closing the door behind her.

Rachel, then, went into her own bedroom, put on her nightclothes, and went out into the living room. She'd been sleeping on the couch since she and Ra'Shaun's father had split up; he'd moved out a few weeks before.

Rachel was glad that she didn't go out; she realized now that she was more tired than she thought. She laid down on the couch with a blanket she'd gotten from her bed.

There wasn't much on T.V. because the cable had been cut off...again.

Rachel watched the 10:00 news. Shortly after that, she started dozing off. Then, she heard a noise.

"Uh-oh," she thought. "That darn mouse again." Then, she thought it could be the neighbor who lived above her. When her neighbor upstairs walked across her floor, Rachel would hear it downstairs. It made kind of a creaking sound.

"I hope it's Miss Lois upstairs." Rachel said to herself. "I don't feel like dealing with that mouse tonight."

Finally, around 12:00 when there was nothing on but infomercials, she got up and turned off the T.V. She laughed at herself as she ran and jumped back on the couch before "the mouse" could get her.

Rachel laid on the couch with her back to the hallway that led to her and Ra'Shaun's bedrooms. She was just beginning to fall asleep when she heard the noise again. Still with her back to the hallway, Rachel slid her foot from under the blanket and stomped hard on the floor. "That should scare the mouse away." She thought. She put her leg back under the blanket and tried to go to sleep. However, the noise kept getting louder, closer even. It even sounded a little different.

Finally, Rachel turned over to face the hallway. Her eyes hadn't adjusted to the complete darkness yet, so she wasn't sure if she was seeing things. Suddenly, her blood ran cold. She saw the figure of a man walking toward her.

"Oh my God!" She screamed as she finally received the message from her brain to get up and run.

She got up to run the ten feet to the door. Just as her hand touched the knob, two arms that felt like a vice closed around her waist. Kicking and fighting for dear life, Rachel was pulled back over to the couch and thrown down violently. When she tried to get up, she felt the back of his hand come slamming down against her cheek. She fell back on to the couch, and before she knew it, he was on top of her holding her down. He sat atop of her just above her knees so that she couldn't kick anymore. He held both of her hands above her head with one hand, and he clamped his other hand over her mouth before she could scream again.

Rachel couldn't believe that this was happening. "How could this be happening? Most of all, why was this happening?" Rachel kept struggling. She could feel herself slipping into darkness. His hand was not only covering her mouth, but also her nose. She almost welcomed the darkness. She wanted to pass out. She wanted to die! Unfortunately, if she did, what would happen to Ra'Shaun? Suddenly, she knew she had to fight for her baby. If she lost consciousness, what would this madman do to her baby?

Then, as if reading her deepest thoughts, he whispered in her ear. "You keep fighting me, and I'm gonna kill your little boy!"

Rachel's whole body froze. She couldn't let anything happen to her son.

"Now, you promise not to scream?" He said.

Rachel quickly shook her in agreement.

He slid his hand down from her nose so that she could breathe, but he made her turn away from him so that she couldn't see his face.

Rachel's mind was screaming. "Who was this man? His voice was so familiar. Did she know him? Did he know her?" That question was answered in the next sentence that came from his mouth.

"Yeah, I've been watching you for a long time, Rachel." He said.

His breath was repulsive, and he smelled very strongly of marijuana.

Rachel tried to turn her head to get a look at him, but as soon as he felt her head begin to turn, his hand came down again across her face.

"Don't look at me, or I will kill you!" He said angrily in her ear.

He began to yank at her clothes. She was only wearing a short Teddy with bikini strap panties. He ripped them off with one rough movement of his hand.

"I know you and your boyfriend broke up, and I know he ain't been livin' here for a while." He said. His voice was dripping with undisguised lust.

"God." Rachel thought silently. "Who is this person, and how does he know so much about me?" She wished with everything inside her that she was going to wake up at any second and realize that it was all a nightmare.

But she didn't wake up. It was really happening. He fumbled around with his pants preparing to penetrate not only her body, but her soul, her dreams, and her sanity.

Rachel tried one last time to get away. She brought her knee up and hit him between his legs, but it was only enough to make him angry. He hit her once more across her face.

"Don't make me kill your son." He threatened.

That was all it took. Rachel decided that if she did what he said, maybe she and Ra'Shaun would live through the night.

So, she let her body go limp. She just laid there totally still.

Finally, he took full pleasure with a body that was unwilling. As he completely violated and defiled her, he continued to whisper in her ear how beautiful she was and how much he loved her.

Tears slid down her face. Suddenly, Rachel remembered that she was no longer taking birth control. What if she became pregnant by a rapist? It would surely be too much for her to bear.

She started to fight again, but he grabbed both her hands and held them over her head again. He didn't withdraw.

"Don't fight me, Rachel; I'm almost done." He growled pressing his face against hers to keep her from looking directly at him. Rachel could feel her face burn from the stubble on his cheek. Her face felt raw.

"I'm gonna get pregnant." She blurted out. "Oh God, please, I'm gonna get pregnant."

This information must have put fear into this madman but not enough to make him stop. He simply withdrew himself from her and spilled his seed right onto her body.

Rachel was so repulsed. She felt the contents of her stomach threatening to rise to her throat. She just laid there and cried. She dared not try to fight again.

Finally, he began to get up, but before he did, he ordered her not to move. Rachel was afraid to disobey him. He told her to turn over onto her stomach. Once she was on her stomach lying face down, he took one of the pillows from the back of the couch and placed it on top of her head.

He held the pillow on top of her head as he got down on his knees and felt underneath the couch with his other hand.

"This is it." Rachel thought. "He's gonna kill me now."

She felt him feeling under the couch. She wondered if he was looking for a knife or a gun.

Suddenly, she felt him remove his hand from the pillow covering her head. She heard him run toward the door. And in what seemed like only a second, he was gone leaving the door wide open.

Rachel jumped up from the couch, still not believing that she and Ra'Shaun were both alive. She ran to his bedroom. He was thankfully still asleep.

She ran to her bedroom and grabbed a robe. She stopped frozen, as she looked over at her bedroom window. It was open. That's how he got in.

Rachel didn't have a phone, so she ran to the next apartment building. She heard a lot of voices inside. She knew the woman who lived there, and it sounded like she was having one of her many card parties.

Rachel banged on the door desperately. She could hear the voices get a little quieter. Finally, the lady who lived there answered the door. Her name was Candy.

Candy opened her door to find her neighbor, Rachel. She looked like she'd been in a fight. Her face was bruised, and she was crying hysterically.

"Rachel, what happened?" Candy asked, shocked at Rachel's appearance.

"I was raped." She answered as she collapsed in a heap in the doorway. She was crying so hard Candy had to ask her to repeat what she'd said.

After Candy realized what Rachel had said, she guided her to her bedroom. Candy sat Rachel down on her bed and held her as one would hold a small child.

"You want me to call the police?" She asked as she rocked Rachel in her arms.

"No." Rachel said suddenly scared again. "Would you call my Mom and Dad?" She said through her tears.

"Sure, what's the number?" She said.

Rachel gave Candy her parents' phone number. She seemed to be almost in shock as she listened to Candy explain who she was, why she was calling so late, and what had happened.

Within minutes, Rachel's parents were at her side. Candy had left Rachel's side only long enough to go back to Rachel's apartment and get Ra'Shaun.

As soon as Rachel's Mom came into the room, Rachel fell into her arms and cried like a baby. It was hard to tell who was crying harder, Rachel, Her Mom, or Candy. Rachel's Father didn't know what to do. He quietly wiped the tears that were falling from his own eyes. He'd never felt so helpless. "Who would do this to his baby girl?"

Finally, Rachel's parents talked her into going to the hospital. Rachel thought back to just a few hours earlier. She was with her family enjoying one of the best Christmases ever.

"Some Christmas." She thought.

Suddenly, Rachel was being shaken awake. Tears were still fresh on her face. It was Mitch. He had picked up the extra key Rachel had left at the front desk for him.

"You all right, baby?" He asked concerned. "What in the world were you dreaming about that would have you crying in your sleep?"

Rachel was so grateful to see his face. She was so grateful that he'd pulled her out of the same nightmare that had controlled her life for years. She threw her arms around his neck and shed a fresh set of tears.

"Shhhh. It's okay, Rach." He soothed.

Mitch held Rachel until she stopped crying.

"You want to tell me about it?" He said gently.

"No, not really, but I think I need to." She said, and with that, she began to tell him the whole story. Rachel had never told anyone outside of her family about why she hated Christmas so much, except Hannah of course, She had definitely never told any other man. She hoped it wouldn't scare Mitch away or change how he felt about her. "Only time will tell." She thought to herself. "Only time will tell."

CHAPTER THIRTEEN

Rachel stood out on the Portside watching crew members come aboard. Some lived off the ship. Some had just gotten away from ship life for a while. She had gotten up a half hour early just so she could come out for some fresh air. This was fast becoming her favorite place on the entire ship, especially when the ship was underway.

Rachel's mind kept returning back to the day she'd told Mitch about the rape. If she'd had any doubt about the way he would react, she had been pleasantly surprised. He'd become even more attentive, actually possessive, and Rachel reveled in it.

Sometimes, it did bother her when she felt like Mitch didn't trust her. Like last week when he had duty and she went to Tradewinds with the girls. She asked Mitch earlier if he would mind if she hung out with her friends. She was beginning to feel like whether she was on or off the ship, she was always with him and only him. Not that she didn't love every minute she spent with him, but she realized that she never really spent much time with her friends anymore. Plus, she was starting to get complaints from the girls about it.

Mitch was in duty section three, and Rachel was in one. Rachel had stood duty on Monday, and Mitch went out with his friends. She didn't have a problem with that. But now that it was his duty day and she was going out with her friends, his whole attitude had changed.

When Rachel asked Mitch if he minded if she hung-out with her friends, he said, "Go on, I don't care." But he said it like he cared very much, and she could tell that he was mad. However, Rachel took it in stride and went any way. Nevertheless, she couldn't enjoy herself knowing that Mitch had a problem with her going out. So, she stayed at the club for only an hour; then, she took a cab back to the ship. Needless to say, her friends were not happy. They were already complaining that Rachel was letting Mitch control her life, but actually, Rachel felt like her life hadn't started until Mitch entered it.

Secretly Rachel believed that they were actually jealous of she and Mitch, and they would love to find something wrong with their relationship. The old "Misery loves company" and all.

Now that Rachel thought about it, none of the relationships that her friends were in were panning out except for maybe Hannah and Melissa. Regardless, they were her friends just the same, so Rachel just figured that she needed to be more patient where they were concerned.

Rachel still couldn't understand why Mitch was so jealous and possessive. Anything he asked her to do, she did it, and anything he told her not to do, she didn't. When she thought about it, it did seem a little drastic sometimes, but the things Mitch taught her, no other man had ever bothered to teach her. So, she was just grateful that he cared so much.

Mitch had told Rachel that the reason he was so jealous, was because he'd been cheated on before, and he loved her so much that he didn't want to lose her. He'd told her that he didn't even like it when other men looked at her. He required her to sit a certain way. He didn't like her to sit with her legs apart while she was on the Mess Decks eating or anywhere else even, and especially with pants on. He claimed that other guys could see the shape and form of her vagina, and he didn't want other M...F...'ers looking at his stuff.

Mitch even had Rachel standing a particular way. One day, Rachel was standing on the Mess Decks talking to Hannah. Shortly into the conversation, about nothing in particular, Hannah noticed that Mitch was coming down passageway behind Rachel.

"Here comes your baby." Hannah said.

Rachel never turned around. She knew how Mitch was. If she'd turned around, he would have known that Hannah had told her of his presence, and he would have reacted negatively. So, Rachel just continued her conversation.

Suddenly, she felt Mitch come up next to her. He took his nails and dug them into Rachel's arm while whispering into her ear.

"Is there a reason why you got your ass cocked?" He said.

Rachel had been standing with her weight on one foot and her arms folded across her chest listening to whatever story Hannah was telling. Even though she was sure that his nails were digging into her flesh deep enough to draw blood, she knew not to let on to her friend what Mitch was doing, or she'd be in more trouble later. So, she smiled sweetly, as if Mitch had just whispered some intimate secret into her ear.

She slowly shifted her weight equally onto both feet, stood up straight, and slid her arms down from her chest. She folded her arms behind her back and covered her behind with her hands.

Afterward, Mitch said a very polite "What's up, Hannah?" He walked away. Rachel continued with her conversation with Hannah, never missing a beat, and her friend was none the wiser.

Rachel's mind returned to the present as she noticed a familiar form coming down the pier. It was Mitch, and he was walking with Londa and her part-time boyfriend, Robert. However, what really caught her attention was the fourth person in the group, Adrian Allen. Adrian had liked Mitch for a long time, and Rachel had known it from day one.

Automatically her mind wondered if she had anything to worry about. She had heard many rumors about Mitch, but whenever she'd asked him about them, he would always be able to explain it all away. Sometimes, he even got mad at Rachel for asking about some of the rumors. He actually seemed wounded that she would even need to question his loyalty.

Rachel was sure he would be able put her mind at ease about this too, although she couldn't begin to imagine why he would be coming onto the ship in the morning. Regardless, she was going to question him just the same.

Rachel left the Portside and went into the skin of the ship to go have breakfast, but after seeing what she'd just seen, she didn't think she'd be able to get anything past the huge lump in her stomach.

CHAPTER FOURTEEN

Rachel wove her way through the crowded Mess Decks and up ladders to 3rd Div. As she stepped on to the Boat Deck, she almost collided with Seaman Mullen.

"Hi Rachel." He said with a smile.

Hank Mullen was the type of person whom everybody liked. He was nice to everyone and always had a kind word.

"Hey Hank, sorry I almost knocked you down." Rachel admitted shyly.

"That's okay, I guess I should have been looking where you were going." He said smiling.

"Yeah, the best way to avoid an accident is to avoid me. That's why my family calls me Clumsy Smurf." They both laughed.

"Well look at it this way. God is the only perfect being in this world, so if the only negative thing anyone can say about you is that you're clumsy, so be it." He said.

"Hank, you are so good for my ego, and I'll remember those wise words the next time I trip over my own shadow, as I so often do."

Rachel said smiling as she began to walk away. However, Hank stopped her by touching her arm and saying. "You know, I believe you are your worst critic. You really should have more confidence in yourself."

"Like I said, you are great for my ego." She was still smiling as she came upon Mitch. Rachel knew right away that something was wrong. His eyes that were usually a beautiful golden brown were now a stormy dark green. She wondered what in the world could have him so upset this early in the day. She didn't have long to find out.

"What the hell did that punk say that got you smiling so hard? And how long y'all been on a first name basis?" He said with a look that literally stopped Rachel in her tracks.

Rachel was thankful that no one else was close enough to hear. She didn't want anyone to see her grovel like she always did whenever she did something that displeased Mitch. But then again, he would never let anyone else see how he treated her behind closed doors, or so she thought.

"Hank has always called me by my first name Mitch, and I've always called him by his." Rachel said.

"Yeah, cause he probably trying to get into your pants." He said barely able to contain his anger.

"Mitch, Hank is probably one of the few guys on this ship that hasn't tried to get with me."

"Yeah, well you was smiling hard about something." He argued back.

"I almost bumped into him when I came through the hatch, and we were laughing about my nickname, Clumsy Smurf."

By now, Mitch had begun to walk away from Rachel, and she was following him pleading her case.

"Yeah, I hear you, Rach." He said never turning around to acknowledge that she was almost running to keep up with him.

"It's true, Mitch. Why would I flirt with someone else right in your face?" Rachel was almost in tears by now.

"Oh, so you would flirt behind me back! He threw back purposely keeping her off balance.

"No, you know me better than that, Mitch! I thought you trusted me."

"I don't trust no damn body, not even my own Mom." He said as he again walked away to go and get more tools.

Rachel just stared at him like he was someone she didn't recognize. When he returned, he looked at her with disgust.

"Don't you have work to do?" He said with his voice dripping with contempt.

Again, Rachel just looked at him trying to find the man she loved so much. "Yeah, but I wanted to finish talking about this first. I don't see where I did anything wrong."

She said, tears flowing freely down her face now. She absently wiped them away.

"Well, if you don't think you did nothin' wrong, carry your ass on then!" He ordered loudly so that anyone on the Boat Deck would hear.

Rachel was so embarrassed by his outburst that she just walked away defeated. Mitch had been acting differently ever since she'd asked him why he was coming onto the ship in the morning when he slept on the ship.

He'd given some excuse about going out to Frank's car and getting his I.D. that he'd left the day before. Rachel wanted so badly to believe him, but there was a bad feeling she got in the pit of her stomach every time she remembered just how chummy he and Adrian had looked that morning. He said she just happened to be walking up the pier to the ship at the same time, so she ran and caught up with Mitch, Londa, and Robert.

When asked, Londa kind of side stepped the question saying that when she looked up Mitch and Adrian were walking along side of her and Robert. She really didn't deny nor confirm the story, but Rachel fully understood.

Although Londa and Rachel were friends, Londa had been friends with Mitch long before Rachel had come to the ship. So, Rachel respected that friendship.

She also hoped that Londa wouldn't tell Mitch that she had questioned her about it after Mitch had already told her what happened. That would give him a whole other reason to be mad at her. Rachel felt like her whole world stopped spinning whenever Mitch was upset with her. She hoped this time it wouldn't last long.

"What y'all arguing about now?" Hannah asked as Rachel climbed up on one of the workboats to assist her with the job she was working on.

"Nothing," Rachel said. She could hear the impatience in Hannah's voice. Hannah cared about both Rachel and Mitch, but she no longer thought they made the ideal couple. Mitch was too possessive and too controlling, and Hannah knew for a fact that he'd hit Rachel before.

"People don't usually cry over nothing, Rach. Why do you put up with his abuse?" She'd finally asked the question everyone on the whole ship had wanted to know for almost a year now.

"Abuse?" Rachel said the word as if it burned her tongue. "Where in the world did you get that from?" She asked completely amazed that Hannah would say such a thing about Mitch.

"Rach, I know Mitch has hit you before, more than once, so don't deny it." Hannah said. "And he treats you like he can't stand you sometimes. You deserve better. You seemed better off when you were waiting for the invisible Corey."

"Oh my God, Hannah, you were the one so gung-ho on me talking to Mitch and leaving Corey alone." Rachel sobbed. "I swear I don't know who to listen to anymore." She sat down in one of the seats of the boat and just let the dam break, holding all the pain frustration she'd been feeling for days. She got up, went over to Fulton, and asked if she could go to the head.

"Sure Tiegs, you all right?" He asked genuinely concerned.

"Yeah, I just need to go get some air." She lied.

Fulton knew the whole story about Mitch and Rachel also. Who in the Deck Dept berthing didn't? He probably knew more than Rachel did. He also felt torn between his loyalty for Mitch and his compassion for Rachel. She was such a kind young lady, and she deserved much more than Mitch was giving her. Still, Fulton also felt an unspoken loyalty for Mitch. He'd been the one who trained Mitch when he first stepped foot on the USS Pennington. Mitch was like a younger brother to Fulton. He was also a very good and dependable worker. However, Mitch had a thing for pretty girls, and it would seem that Rachel was one girl on the ship whom every guy noticed and liked. Mitch had her. The only thing was he didn't know how to treat her.

"We'll be breaking for lunch in about twenty minutes anyway; so, go ahead and leave now." He said. "I'll see you after lunch."

"Thanks, Fulton." Rachel said gratefully. She left the Boat Deck not knowing that Mitch's eyes were on her the whole time. He was already feeling badly about the way he'd treated her. He wasn't even really mad at her. He was mad at himself. He never had any intention of really starting a relationship with Rachel. He wanted to prove something to Frank and all the others, that he could actually possess her. He thought he could "hit it and run," without getting his heart involved. However, Rachel was as beautiful inside as she was outside. She had the most remarkable way of making him feel like he could tell her anything and not worry about it coming back to him later from someone else, only different than the way he first told it.

Mitch had completely fallen for Rachel, and it hurt to see her so upset, especially when he knew that he was the cause of her pain. More than anything right now, he just wanted to hold her. He was still surprised that he reacted the way he did. All he knew was that he did love Rachel, but it seemed that the more he admitted that fact to himself, the worse he treated her. Then, after hurting her, he'd worry about her leaving him. That thought scared him more than anything.

He couldn't imagine not having her to talk to, to hold, or to love. Nevertheless, the thought that scared him most was imagining Rachel in the arms of someone else. Mitch tried to put his mind off Rachel and on his job. He only

had a few more minutes until lunch. Then, he would call
Rachel, apologize, and make everything right.

CHAPTER FIFTEEN

Rachel was sitting in the Crew's Lounge on a Sunday morning, reading one of her many romance novels. Although the book was open and her eyes were scanning the words on the page. She had no idea what she had read for the past two paragraphs. She couldn't stop thinking about last weekend. She'd gone home for the weekend to surprise her Mom of her birthday.

She hadn't realized how much she'd missed her family, especially Ra'Shaun. Seeing her little boy was the best part of the whole weekend. The second best was the fact that Mitch went with her. Rachel still couldn't believe that he actually went home with her. She wondered if it was as significant to him as it was to her. She hoped so. Her whole family loved him from the minute they met him. Her sisters all thought he was gorgeous. Rachel wondered if they would all feel the same way if they knew that just two days ago Mitch had beat her up pretty badly, all because they had gone to a club and some guy Rachel didn't even know touched her butt. Mitch had been walking right behind her, so she just assumed it had been him. He claimed that Rachel knew it wasn't him. He slapped her around a few times. By the time he was done, Rachel was sporting a swollen, busted lip, and a few sore ribs. He apologized through tears and swore he would never hit her again. He could be so charming and loving; it was hard for Rachel to stay mad at him.

Ra'Shaun practically followed Mitch everywhere he went. Rachel's brother Greg also took a strong liking to Mitch. As soon as Greg had Mitch alone, he pounced and asked him if he wanted to go and "smoke some killer?"

Mitch looked at Rachel. "You don't mind do you?" He asked.

"Go ahead." She said. Rachel knew that Greg was testing Mitch to see how "cool" he was, and Mitch passed with flying colors.

Greg took Mitch to the only bar that existed in Salem. Mitch was high practically the whole weekend, thanks to Greg. Rachel worried about Mitch's number being called for a drug test when they got back to the ship. If he tested positive for drugs, it could be the end of his Navy career.

A few days after Rachel and Mitch returned from Jersey, rumors started floating about an upcoming cruise. No one really knew where to, but everyone was speculating.

The crew didn't have to wait long. The next week, Deck Dept got the official word, from BMC Edwards, that the rumors were true. The USS Pennington and her crew would be leaving for a two-month cruise to Bergen, Norway, in the North Atlantic.

The ship would be pulling out the second week in October and returning the second week in December.

No one seemed at all happy about the cruise, not to mention that they'd all be underway during Thanksgiving. Rachel, on the other hand, was taking it all in stride. She looked at the upcoming cruise as some romantic getaway for her and Mitch.

She couldn't wait to finally have Mitch to herself. There would be no phone calls from Becca about wanting to come and visit him in Norfolk anymore. Whenever Mitch talked to Becca, she would talk about transferring her job as a manager at a clothing store in Ohio, to Norfolk.

Just the thought of having to compete with another woman for Mitch scared Rachel to death, although she competed everyday with the other four hundred women on the ship. Rachel wondered what she'd do if Becca did come to live in Norfolk. Mitch had told Rachel from the beginning how very jealous and possessive Becca was. Rachel had decided that she wasn't about to go through the same crazy drama she'd went through with Wayne's ex. "But then again, Becca is white." She thought as she laughed to herself. "How tough can she be?"

Rachel looked up from her book and smiled as she saw Londa come into the lounge with Karen Shorter. Karen was quickly becoming one of the girls. She was about 5'10." Her skin was a smooth dark, chocolate brown. Although Karen was tall and dark skinned, she was a very pretty girl. She was 21-years-old and had also gotten to the ship a few months before Hannah and Rachel.

There was only one thing that Rachel didn't care for about Karen and that was the fact that Karen dated "other than black" men. Rachel didn't have a problem with interracial dating, but she didn't like that Karen didn't want anything to do with black men at all. Other than that, she was a gem and a close, loyal friend with a deep Kentucky accent and a heart of pure gold.

"Dag girl, we been lookin' all over the ship for you." Londa said. "I don't know what made me decide to come down here to look for you; you never come down here."

"I know. I just wanted to do some reading. It was a little too loud in the berthing, even with my headphones on." Rachel said.

"You comin' to brunch with us?" Karen asked.

"Nah, I'm not really hungry. I'll probably see you guys at lunch."

"But Hannah and Melissa are already up there waiting for us." Karen said. "Besides, you know you always eat lunch with Ghram."

Rachel didn't miss the slight hint of an attitude from Karen, which was unusual for her. Rachel just chocked it up to jealousy because she and Mitch were doing so well, and Karen was in between men. All the rumors that Mitch liked to run this girl and that girl had not been lost on her, but Rachel felt she had no reason to believe that

Mitch was unfaithful to her. He constantly told her that he never wanted to lose her and that if he couldn't have her no one could. They'd been together for over a year now, and she just couldn't see herself with anyone else.

"You are allowed to eat lunch with someone else other than Mitch Ghram you know!" Karen said, this time without even an attempt to hide her displeasure with Rachel.

"Really, well thank you for your permission, Karen. I've been hoping that one day I could eat lunch with someone other than Mitch." Rachel added her own sarcasm. Tired of the attack that felt she didn't deserve, Rachel finally asked, "What is your problem, Karen?"

"I don't have a problem." Karen stated. "But if Mitch can do whatever he wants, I don't see why you can't too."

"Well, that's just it," Rachel said very calmly. "I am doing what I want. I want to read, so that's what I'm doing. Now, if my reading right now instead of going to chow with you is going to cause you to have a nervous breakdown, I'll put the book away." Rachel said laughing and attempting to lighten the mood, but Karen didn't bite.

"Whatever Rach, do what you want. Can't nobody tell you nothing since got with Mitch." Karen said as she walked out the lounge leaving Rachel wondering what had just happened.

Rachel looked at Londa who had been quiet during the whole strange conversation, but Rachel also noticed that she didn't seem surprised by the whole exchange either.

"Damn, who the hell pissed in her Cheerios this morning cause I know it wasn't me." Rachel said."

"Girl, don't pay Karen no mind; she just PMSing about the North Atlantic cruise like everybody else." Londa said.

"I'll see you at lunch time, that's if I get up out my rack in time. You know me, once I get my belly full, I'm down for the count." Londa joked.

"See you later." Rachel said back as Londa walked out of the lounge.

Londa felt torn about the exchange she'd just witnessed. She knew exactly what was wrong with Karen. She'd heard the same rumor that Rachel and the rest of the ship had heard. Mitch was already cheating on Rachel. "Knowing Mitch's record, it was probably true." Londa thought to herself.

"Oh well, she said to herself. I'm not getting in it. Mitch is my friend and so is Rachel. Besides if he does it long enough, she'll find out, but knowing Rachel, it probably won't change a thing." Londa thought to herself as she headed on up to the Mess Decks to have brunch with the girls.

CHAPTER SIXTEEN

Rachel watched as the wake from the huge vessel she was on flowed away from her. She only had one hour left on her watch. She was glad that she was on watch alone, and she didn't have anyone standing UI with her on this watch. It seemed strange that only a year ago she was the one standing UI. Now, she was the one in the position to teach.

The whole three hours she had been on the fantail. The Port and Starboard watches had decided that they didn't want to rotate on this watch. That was fine with Rachel. She just wanted to be alone, watch the waves, and try to file away everything that had taken place in the past few days.

It was such a bitter cold. The North Atlantic had not been kind to the USS Pennington and her crew. Rachel still couldn't fathom why their captain would bring the crew of the USS Pennington to somewhere so bleak. Bergen, Norway, in her opinion, left much to be desired. She would much rather be back in Norfolk and the cool, gentle winters there. She now understood why none of the crew wanted to come here. They'd been in Norway for two months already, and they still weren't leaving for three more days. They were awaiting supplies, and they were late.

Rachel took a deep breath and blew out a cloud of fog. She hated the cold, always had. She missed her family. She'd gotten a letter from oldest sister, Sharon. Sharon was practically begging her to come home for Christmas. She went through all the usual hobnob about it not being about Rachel, but about the birth of Jesus, Blah, blah, blah.

Rachel wondered if she was gonna have to go through this every year. "Why don't they just leave me alone?" She thought to herself. Regardless, deep down, she knew they all loved her very much, and they meant well.

Rachel really did want to go home, especially after this particular cruise. This would definitely qualify as one of the most traumatic experiences of her life. Not shortly after the ship left Norway, on the way back home, problems arose. These problems could have been avoided had the captain stuck to the original course.

One night around 22:00 hours, the USS Pennington received a distress call from another ship. A Dutch ship that had run aground. Normally protocol would demand that the USS Pennington keep on her mission to Norfolk and send help back because it was not a US ship. Unfortunately, Captain Russell decided to go and help himself. He put the USS Pennington at risk because they'd just narrowly escaped the same storm that had caused the Dutch ship to run aground and was still very much in the middle of the storm.

After arriving at the place where the troubled ship was, things were worse than expected. The waves were so rough and high that while Rachel was on watch on the bridge, the waves actually slammed against the windows… eight decks above water level. Rachel was afraid for the first time since she'd been aboard the Sound. She started thinking about movies like the "Titanic," and "The Poseidon Adventure."

She finally realized that this ship was no different than those. It was made of very heavy metal, and it could sink just like any other vessel. When she was relieved from her watch on the bridge, she couldn't get down to the berthing quickly enough. She needed someone to calm her nerves, and no one could do that like her best friend, Hannah. When Rachel got down to the berthing, she was alarmed at how loud it was. Everyone was scared. The ship was being tossed to and fro like a toy. Rachel went over to Hannah's rack. Hannah was just sitting there staring off into space. Rachel sat down on the rack next to her. Her friend didn't seem in any position to calm anyone's nerves.

"Hannah, you O.K.?" Rachel asked quietly.

Slowly Hannah seemed to register the familiar voice. Suddenly she grabbed Rachel, threw her arms around her, and collapsed into tears.

"Oh my God, Rachel, I'm so scared." She said, going from eerily quiet to almost hysterical in the blink of an eye.

"I know." Rachel said. "I'm scared too."

"No, I mean Evan is back on the Fantail. All the guys from Deck Dept are back there." She said between tears.

"But why are the deck guys back there?" Rachel asked.

"I don't know." Hannah sobbed. "I just know that they won't let nobody back there; I'm scared for Evan."

"Is Mitch back there too?" Rachel finally asked the question she'd wanted to ask, but afraid to know the answer.

"Yeah Rach, all of them are back there. First, Second, and Third Division." She said.

Before Hannah could say another word, the collision alarm was sounded.

"Oh my God." Both girls cried almost in unison.

They knew things were really bad if they were setting off the collision alarm. All they could do was hold each other and cry. A few minutes later an announcement came over the one M.C. that every crew member dreaded to hear, one that almost made Rachel's blood run cold.

"Man overboard, Man overboard."

Rachel couldn't believe her ears. "Was this really happening?"

"Dear God," she prayed silently to herself. "Please let Mitch be safe." But as quickly as that thought came, it was replaced by "How can I possibly ask God for anything?" She was suddenly filled with shame. She faintly remembered one of the scriptures of The Bible. It was something about "My sheep know my voice." How would she ever know His voice if she never listened when He spoke, and even more than that, how would He ever recognize her voice if she only talked to Him in times of trouble? She silently bargained that if God brought her out of this, she would pray more.

As it would turn out, Rachel's life was spared as were Hannah, Evan, Mitch, Frank, and everyone else in Deck Dept. Still, there had been a man lost over the side. His name was Petty Officer Andrew Frank. Although Petty Officer Frank wasn't actually a part of Deck Dept, his workstation was on the Boat Deck because he was a diver.

As a matter of fact, Andrew and Rachel had been working together that very same morning. They had been tending the same tag line while the dive boat was being lowered into the water. Although Rachel didn't know him very well, Andrew seemed like a very quiet, but nice guy. He was only 21-years-old, and his mother's only child. Rumor had it that he'd just gotten engaged before the ship left Norfolk to his baby's mother. His baby was only 3-months-old.

Petty Officer Frank had fallen over the side at approximately 12:15 a.m. Over four hours had passed before he was pulled out of the icy waters by a helicopter. Still another four hours went by before the Captain came on the one M.C. and announced, "Petty Officer Frank is dead. That is all."

He sounded as cold and unfeeling as the freezing water from which Andrew had been pulled. It's not like the crew didn't already know that Andrew was dead. "How could anyone survive the waters of the North Atlantic for over four hours?" Still, the Capt spoke as if he were talking about the weather.

From the moment Andrew's death was officially announced, a very deep sadness fell over the crew. Rachel herself even felt a sense of loss. She was sitting on the Mess Decks with Mitch and other members of Deck Dept, along with other people who knew and loved

Andrew Frank when the announcement came. To Rachel's surprise, Mitch who was sitting across from her holding both her hands in his, immediately broke down and wept like a baby. Suddenly burst of wailing and sobbing completely replaced heavy silence, as everyone who had been waiting finally got the news that they'd known was inevitable.

All thoughts of fraternization were lost to everyone as they embraced, held one another, and mourned together.

As Rachel relived the scene in her mind, tears rolled down her cheek. Although she didn't know Andrew well, she still hurt for his mother and his fiancée. She also hurt for Mitch because he did know him. Even though he could seem cold and mean sometimes, Rachel knew that there was another side to him, a side that he seemed to show only to her. Unfortunately, whenever she witnessed this loving caring side of him, it was usually after he'd been very mean or even physical with her. Nevertheless, it didn't matter as long as she did get to see this side of him more than the other side, and for the most part, she did.

CHAPTER SEVENTEEN

Rachel sat with her hands folded on the table in front of her. She was determined to give the impression that she was not intimidated, although if someone had said "Boo" in a voice even slightly above a whisper, she probably would have burst into tears.

She had been preparing for this day for eight months, and she knew everything there was to know about being a Dental Tech.

Rachel had done over 300 O.J.T. hours, and she knew the Dental Rate Book inside out. Now, all she had to do was sit in front of eight chiefs and officers and answer one question from each one about the Dental field to their satisfaction.

She was now down to the last person, Lt. Commander Braxton. Rachel felt like she could finally exhale. Lt. Commander Braxton was the Dept Head of the Dental Dept. Rachel felt like she was home free. Braxton always liked Rachel. Rachel had assisted her quite a few times.

Rachel knew that Lt. Commander Braxton wouldn't give her a hard question. So, she waited for the last question, and when it came, she wished she were close enough to kick Commander Braxton in the shin.

"Seaman Tiegs, my question is easy enough." She said. "Why do you want to be a Dental Tech?"

"How in the world could she possibly think that this was an easy question?" Rachel thought as she felt the blood drain from her face. She took a deep breath, told herself to talk slowly and clearly, and just to tell the truth.

"Well ma'am, I want to help people. I want to know that at the end of the day that I made a difference in someone's life, even if it was only by calming them down so that we could get them out of pain. It would make me feel very satisfied. Plus, I find the Dental Field very fascinating." She answered.

"Thank you Seaman Tiegs." Lt. Commander Braxton said with a smile that revealed nothing. "If you could wait outside for a minute, we'd like to discuss your answers. We'll call you back in shortly and give you our decision."

"Yes ma'am." Rachel said as she stood up and left the room.

Rachel stood out in the hall for what seemed like forever, when in all actuality, it was only twelve minutes.

"Seaman Tiegs, you can come back in now." One of the officers stuck his head out the room and said, bringing Rachel out of her daze.

"Thank you." Rachel said as she walked pass the officer and back to her seat.

"Seaman Tiegs," The Supply Chief said. "After going over the answers you gave, reviewing your O.J.T., and discussing the whole rate change, we all agree that you should remain in Deck Dept for the remainder of the month. Then, you can begin checking out of Deck Dept and into Dental Dept on the first of April." He smiled as he saw the restraint Rachel was trying so hard to maintain. "I assume you're all right with our decision."

"Yes sir." Rachel said as she walked around, shook each person's hand, and thanked each one personally.

As Rachel walked back down to the berthing to go change her uniform, she couldn't wait to tell Mitch. She hoped he would be proud of her. She felt proud of herself. She could actually see herself going so much further than Deck Dept, not that there was anything wrong with Deck.

Still, Rachel felt like if she used her brain more, she wouldn't have to use her back at all. There was no reason she couldn't go as far as her brain could take her. Bull work was for men, not women, and Rachel had no intention of doing Bull work any longer than the last day of March.

CHAPTER EIGHTEEN

Rachel awoke with a start at the sound of the Reveille call. Normally, she'd be awake at least 15 minutes before, but she'd had trouble sleeping. She was certain not too many people on the ship had gotten any ship. Everyone was wondering what the next few weeks would reveal.

There had been a lot of talk about the U.S. going to war with Iraq. Just the word war scared Rachel completely to death. The only thing she knew about war was that people died, and the world was never the same.

Rachel got up from her rack, going through her normal routine in a total haze. She wondered what the next few weeks would bring. She remembered the stories she'd heard people tell of Vietnam. "Would it be anything like that?"

What scared her the most was the fact that if the U.S. went to war, the USS Pennington would be leaving for Saudi Arabia and Bahrain within the month. Rachel brushed her shoulder length hair as she looked into the mirror and saw nothing.

She was in such a daze that she didn't realize that someone else had entered the head. Melissa had been standing next to Rachel for a few minutes now. She'd said good morning to her, and Rachel had yet to respond.

"Hello." Melissa said as she waved her hand in front of Rachel's face to get her attention. "Anybody home?"

"Oh, hey Lissa." Rachel said void of any emotion.

"What's wrong with you, Rach?" She asked genuinely concerned. "You actin like a space cadet. You and Mitch having problems?"

"No, me and Mitch are not having problems. Why do you ask?" Rachel said annoyed that her friend just automatically assumed that something was wrong with her relationship with her boyfriend.

"Okay." Melissa said. "Down boy. I just asked you a simple question, because you seem so quiet, but I won't ask you nothing else." She said as she turned to leave.

"Lissa, I'm sorry." Rachel said realizing how she must have sounded. "Me and Mitch really are fine. I'm just trying to wrap my mind around the fact that we might really be going to war. I mean I never in a million years thought that there would be another war, at least not in my lifetime, and I certainly never thought I would be a part of it. I'm really scared."

"I know." Melissa said, suddenly understanding completely how Rachel was feeling.

"I'm scared to death too. But we're supposed to lean on each other when we're scared, not eat each other alive." She laughed.

Rachel laughed too. She hugged her friend. "You always know how to make me laugh." Rachel said. "I really am sorry for snapping at you."

"It's all right; I know you didn't mean it." Melissa said. "You and Hannah want to go up and get some chow?"

"Nah, I'm not hungry, but Hannah might." She said.

"Okay, I'll see you up on the Mess Decks at lunch time." Melissa said. "And try not to worry til we have something to worry about. Deal?" She wanted to put her friend at ease, but she was pretty sure after talking to Fulton last night that the U.S. would soon be going to war with Iraq.

"Deal." Rachel said as she left the head. She didn't really feel any better than she had before talking to Melissa. Nevertheless, her friend was right. There was no sense getting all worked up until she knew she had a reason.

Rachel still seemed to be deep in thought. People passed her and spoke. She responded automatically, but she really didn't see or hear anyone. She kept walking not even realizing where she was going until she arrived at the Main Deck, Portside. This seemed to be the place her heart led her whenever she was bothered by one thing or another.

As Rachel looked down at the different people coming aboard, she thought about how simple her life used to be. She was an uncomplicated Southern Jersey country girl. All she ever wanted out of life was someone to love who would love her just as much as she loved him. She wanted someone who would cherish her, be faithful to her, never leave her, and never hurt her.

Funny, as she thought of this perfect person, she realized that there was only one who could fit the bill, Jesus, and it would still be a one-sided relationship because she could never in a million lifetimes love Him as deeply and completely as He loved her. Well, she wasn't really ready for that deep an affair anyway. She smiled to herself just thinking about it.

"Rachel, what you doin' out here?" Mitch said. "Didn't you hear the One MC?"

Rachel turned to look into the face of a confused Mitch.

"He seemed angry, but what else was new?" She thought.

"I'm sorry, Mitch; what did you say?" She said trying to make sense of whatever he was rambling about.

"I said, didn't you hear the "one M.C.?" He said more irritated now. "The Captain wants everyone on the Helo deck, all departments."

"Oh, I did hear the voice, but I didn't really pay attention to what they were saying." She admitted. "I figured it was just the regular announcements."

"No Rachel, it wasn't the regular announcements." He spat out in disgust. "He's probably gonna tell us that we going to war with Iraq. You better get your head out of your ass and pay attention."

"What are you mad at me for?" She asked, hurt by his attitude.

"I'm not mad at you. I'm mad at the whole situation." He said.

"Well, I didn't create the situation. Your President did!" She spat back and walked away.

"Rachel." Mitch called after her, but she kept walking. She knew if she stopped, all she would get was an "I'm sorry," and she'd grown tired of empty apologies. She went on up to the Helo deck, to hear firsthand with everyone else just what the future held for the USS Pennington.

CHAPTER NINETEEN

As it turned out, the war didn't begin, but the USS Pennington had to deploy anyway. The Captain had announced that tensions were running high over in Saudi Arabia and the Sound would be leaving in January for Bahrain.

So, the crew had less than 3 months to get all their personal business in order. Everyone took leave in two separate time periods, so that they could go home and say goodbye to their families. It would be at least six months before they saw their families or the United States again.

Anyone taking leave and going further than 50 miles from the base would be required to report back to the ship no later than Dec. 31.

Rachel nor Mitch had been home in months. Mitch wanted to go home, but after child support and car payments started coming out of his pay, there wasn't even 100.00 dollars per pay left. He'd bought a little

1984 Honda Accord that barely ran. So, Rachel had paid to have his car fixed.

Rachel's paycheck more than tripled Mitch's because she had Ra'Shaun for a dependent, so even though he had the car, she had the finances. So, they compromised.

Although Rachel could afford to fly, rent a car, and drive, she decided to help Mitch get a plane ticket home to Ohio, and he let her use his car to go home to New Jersey.

Secretly, Rachel wanted to use his car anyway; she wanted everyone in Salem to see her driving her man's car, especially Wayne.

Although Rachel was completely in love with Mitch, she still thought of Wayne often. She'd heard that shortly after she'd left for the Navy, he and Rachel were expecting their second child. The news still hurt terribly, but Rachel cared about Wayne so much that all she could do was hope he was happy. She had passed Wayne and Rachel a couple of times while she was home on leave. It didn't escape her attention that he barely spoke when he was with her. It hurt Rachel to think that as close as they were, he would act like she hadn't been important to him at one time. He'd actually looked nervous that Rachel might say more to him than "Hi."

However, Rachel knew how his babies' mother was, and she would never do or say anything to cause any added complication in his life. All Rachel wanted was to come home, see her son, spend time with her family, and go back to V.A. to sail away for ½ a year.

Rachel hadn't had the most enjoyable time while she was home. The nightmares had returned, more vivid that ever. So, although she was going to miss her family very much, she couldn't wait to get back to what she now considered home, Virginia.

Rachel had stayed with her Mom and Dad while she was home, and Ra'Shaun stayed there with her. Two days before she was to leave, Ra'Shaun asked her if he could go with her. Rachel explained to him that she was about to leave on a "big boat" for a long time, but when she returned, she would let him come and visit her in V.A.

Ra'Shaun said that he understood, Rachel knew that he really didn't. She wished with all her heart that she could be the kind of mother Ra'Shaun needed, but she wasn't.

She loved her son dearly, and she felt guilty that he was with his Dad and didn't have mother to love him and be with every day like other 5-year-olds did. Unfortunately, the relationship between Rachel and Ra'Shaun's father was hardly civil, much less loving. They'd actually grown up together and were best friends for years, but now, they could barely stand to be in the same room without arguing.

Rachel never understood why, but Raymond (Ra'Shaun's father) changed drastically after Rachel was raped. He seemed to blame her for it. He even said, "Next time it happens, don't call me." A few weeks after the rape, Rachel moved back to her apt. Raymond was staying with her to "keep her safe," but he treated her so cruel. He let her know at all times that he was only there for Ra'Shaun and that the only feelings he had for her were contempt.

Raymond thought it funny to jump out of a closet or from behind a door and scare Rachel. Because she had been attacked in this apartment, every little noise had her on edge. So, when he pulled these pranks, her nerves were completely shot for the rest of the day. Raymond, however, would fall on the floor laughing. He seemed to get a kick out of seeing the terror on her face.

Rachel never told her family because she knew that her brother, Greg, would beat the life clean out of Raymond, and although there was no love lost between them anymore, he was still Ra'Shaun's father, and he did love his son very much.

Rachel loved her son too, and there had been a huge aching hole in her heart ever since she'd left and been separated from him. Still, she felt that the only way she could hold on to her sanity after the rape was to leave Salem far behind, and that meant leaving everything attached to Salem, including her son.

Rachel honestly felt that Ra'Shaun was better off with Raymond. He was a good father and seemed to always put Ra'Shaun first. Rachel knew that she very seldom did that, even before the rape.

Finally, the day came for Rachel to go back to Virginia. It was Sunday afternoon. Rachel had gone to church with her Mom. She could barely keep her mind on what Pastor Barnes was saying. All she could think about was how much she missed Mitch. She'd called him several times and was concerned that there was never any answer. There was also no answering machine, so she couldn't leave a message for Mitch to let him know that she'd called.

Rachel wondered if Mitch had spent any time with Becca. They were still a couple after all. Rachel felt like she was having an affair with a married man. She could feel her insecurities creeping up on her. "What if Mitch came back and decided to stop seeing her? What if he came back and Becca was with him?"

Rachel was in her old bedroom changing out of her church clothes and into her sweats. She would be leaving shortly, and she wanted to be comfortable on the 4 ½ hour drive back to Norfolk. "Rachel telephone." Her mom called.

Rachel picked up the receiver in her room. "I got it, Mom." She answered back.

"Hello." Rachel said, thinking it was anyone but who it was.

"What's up?" Mitch said.

"Hey." Rachel said with her heart in her throat. He still made her nervous after almost two years.

"God, Mitch, I miss you so much." She gasped.

"Yeah right, that's why you haven't called me not one time in almost two weeks." He said angrily.

"What? Mitch, I've been calling you every day, but I haven't been getting any answer." She whined. "I wanted to leave you a message, but there was no answering machine."

"Now, I know you lying cause we do have an answering machine." He spat back with disgust.

"Mitch! I swear I've been calling you every day, more than once a day." She couldn't believe that he was mad at her. She never seemed to be able to please him, no matter what she did or didn't do.

"Didn't you write the number down that I gave you, or did you forget it?" He asked, still very mad.

"Yeah, I wrote it down, and I have it right here." She called the number out to him.

"Well, no wonder you didn't get me." He said now sounding more annoyed than angry. He told her that she had the last four numbers backwards.

"I'm sorry, but I have been trying to call you every day." Then, she had a thought. "But just the same, you haven't called me the whole time I've been home."

"I'm calling you now ain't I?" He came right back.

"Look here." He said and instantly Rachel's heart sank. Whenever he started a sentence with "look here," it was usually bad news. She braced herself for whatever he was about to say.

"I just wanted to make sure that you knew what time my plane was coming in tomorrow, so I don't have to take a cab." He said. He was actually calm again and didn't seem mad anymore.

"Yeah, I got the information right here. I'll call it out to you to make sure I got it right." Now, she was second guessing herself.

She called out the information to Mitch, and he confirmed that it was right.

"Well I gotta go. I don't want to run up my Mom's phone bill; I don't want to hear her mouth." He said.

Did you have a good time?" She asked. She would have said anything to keep him on the phone. She missed his voice, even if he had been yelling at her.

"Yeah." He said. "But I miss you."

"I miss you too, so much." She said. "I'm so sorry I was calling the wrong number." She was crying now.

"It's okay, baby." He said. "I'm sorry for yelling at you. I gotta go. Don't forget me tomorrow, okay?" He laughed.

"No chance." She laughed back. "See you tomorrow; I love you."

"I love you too." He said. Then, he was gone.

He still loved her. She smiled to herself; that was all that mattered to her. He still loved her, and everything was fine.

When Rachel came out of her room to go put her bags in the car, her mother was waiting in the living room.

"Rachel, are you all right?" She asked concerned. She'd heard most of Rachel's part of the phone conversation because she'd raised her voice almost hysterically. She could look at her daughter and tell that she'd been crying.

"Yeah, I'm okay." She said without looking at her Mother's face. "Mitch just had me upset for a minute." She admitted. "He thought all this time that I never called him."

"But you've been calling him the whole time you've been home. Didn't you tell him that?" Her Mother asked.

"Yeah, but it turns out that I wrote the number down wrong, and I was calling the wrong number the whole time." She said embarrassed.

"Well, that could happen to anybody." Her Mother said.

"Yeah, but if it was gonna happen to anybody, it would be me." She said, angry with herself for being so stupid.

"Well," her Mother said, "I don't remember Mitch blowing up your phone since you've been home." She was angry with Mitch for making her little girl feel like she was a screw up. She was also mad at Rachel for wanting to be with someone like that.

"Mom." Rachel said in her no-nonsense voice. "Let it go."

"Okay, fine." Her Mother said, raising her hands in surrender. "I just want you to be happy. I love you, honey." She said as she took her daughter in her arms and held her tight.

"I know, Mom." Rachel kissed her on the cheek. "I am happy." She said. "Now, give me one last hug so I can go say goodbye to everyone else before I get on the road.

They embraced one last time. Mary Tiegs held her daughter as if she would never see her again.

"I love you, Mom." Rachel said hoping to put her Mother's worries to rest. "I'm okay, really. Try not to worry about me." She pleaded.

"I'll try." She promised, knowing that it was in vain.

"Dad!" Rachel yelled down the hallway toward her parents' bedroom. "I'm leaving now." She said.

Her father came out of the bedroom. He walked up to his daughter and hugged her so tight that Rachel could barely breathe. He pulled back but rested his hands on her shoulders.

"Do you have enough money?" He asked.

"Yeah Daddy, I'm fine, thank you. I love you." Rachel said with tears in her eyes. Take care of Mom and make her keep promise not to worry."

"I'll try." He said with tears threatening to spill from his eyes.

"Funny, that's the same thing she said." Rachel said.

"Well, I'm gonna go say bye to my sisters and my brother and make one last stop to see Ra'Shaun. I'll call you when I get to V.A." She said.

Her parents walked her to the car, gave her one last hug, and waved as she drove away.

Rachel drove off, letting the tears flow freely. She went by Gloria's house. Her other two sisters, Sharon and Diane were there to say goodbye along with all their kids. Sharon said a prayer for Rachel and asked God to protect her and her entire ship's crew while they were out of the country and to bring them all back safely. Again, there wasn't a dry eye in the house when she left.

She could barely see through the tears when she left her brother's house. She loved her family so much, and she would miss them terribly. She stopped at Raymond's house and said goodbye to Ra'Shaun. He'd drawn a picture of him and her. She promised that she would hang it in her rack so that she could think about him every night before she fell asleep and every morning when she woke up.

"I love you, Mommy." He said in the sweetest voice.

"I love you too." Rachel said through tears. "I'll miss you, but I'll be back as soon as it gets hot outside, and you get out of school, okay?"

"Okay." He said. "Bye Mommy."

"Bye sweetheart." Rachel said as she held him one last time. She waved at him once more as she drove away.

She wiped the tears from her face as she looked in her rearview mirror. She took a deep breath, pulled out onto the highway, and began her count down of her 4 ½ hour drive home.

CHAPTER TWENTY

The ship had been out to sea for over two months now. Most of the time had been spent underway. The ship had only stopped at two ports. One port was Bahrain, and the other was Italy to refuel. The USS Pennington was now on its way to Alexandria, Spain. They would be there for ten days, so the crew would actually get a chance to have some fun.

Rachel was so excited about seeing Spain. She didn't really know what to expect, but no one did; that's what made it so exciting. While the ship was in Bahrain, no one was allowed to leave, and they were actually anchored out about thirty minutes away from land.

Since no one could go anywhere, most everyone still had all of their paychecks. Rachel couldn't wait to go shopping with her friends; it was all they talked about.

The first day the ship pulled into Spain, Mitch had duty, so he couldn't leave. Rachel knew if she left without him all hell would break loose, so she told him that she had to perm her hair and that she wouldn't be leaving the ship til the next day with him. Of course, he went through the usual "Go ahead with your girls. I don't mind," knowing it was a lie. However, Rachel knew better. Besides, she really did have to perm her hair. She wanted to look her best when she left the ship with Mitch the next day.

She knew there were so many girls who would give their right arm to be with Mitch. Rachel felt so privileged to be the one he'd chosen. She'd never loved anyone the way she loved him. She let him completely lead and change her life, and she had to admit that most of the changes, she loved.

She liked the way he followed her with his eyes whenever they were in the same room. She appreciated little things like, the way he taught her to say, "I have to go to the bathroom" instead of "I have to go pee." Even now to think of that fateful lesson, made her laugh to herself.

Rachel remembered it like it was just a few minutes ago. She and Mitch were standing outside of her berthing area. They were saying goodbye for the evening, and

Rachel was about to go downstairs but before she did. She unfortunately muttered, "I have to go pee."

She watched his whole expression change, but she didn't understand why. Well, she was soon to find out.

"You don't tell nobody you gotta go pee. You just say you have to go to the bathroom. You supposed to be a lady; you don't need to tell everybody what you gonna do when you get to the bathroom. You just let them know that you need to go there. You understand? I don't ever wanna hear you say that no more."

Rachel felt like she had just been reprimanded by her Dad, and she would have been embarrassed had she been given enough time to be. However, before her face could turn the proper shade of red, another sailor came walking pass Mitch and Rachel and exclaimed loudly as she did, "I gotta pee like a big ole dog!"

It was all Rachel who could not help but burst into tears laughing, but she knew if she did, Mitch would have a fit. Mitch just looked at Rachel and said, "Now how that sound, a female talking bout she gotta pee like a big ole dog?"

Again, Rachel kept her composure, barely told Mitch good night, ran down stairs, and fell on her rack laughing. Hannah came over and asked her what was so funny. When Rachel finally got herself together, she told her, and they laughed for the next half hour. Even now, Rachel wondered why her Mom never taught her something like that. Although she did love the things that Mitch taught her, there were still some things that she wished she could change about him like that dark side no one liked, including Rachel. But as long as she was careful not to make him angry, the "Dark Mitch" pretty much stayed away.

Rachel heard the phone ring in the lounge of the berthing where she slept. Mitch had already called for her twice, and James had already called for Londa once. She wondered whose boyfriend it was this time.

"Rachel Tiegs!" Someone yelled from the lounge area. "Phone!"

"Coming!" Rachel yelled back. "Oh God, here it comes." She thought. "I'm gonna have to hear his mouth cause I'm not ready."

"Hello, this is Tiegs." Rachel said with more confidence than she actually felt.

"Hey baby, me and James gonna go on down and meet you and Londa on the pier." Mitch said without the slightest hint of an attitude.

She was shocked. "Okay, we're almost ready." Rachel said.

"About how much longer y'all gonna be?" He asked, still being very patient.

"No more than fifteen minutes." She answered.

"All right, we'll be waiting down there." He said.

"Okay, we'll be right behind you." Rachel answered; then, she hung up.

As she went back over to her rack, she couldn't help but smile. She was so excited about finally spending time with Mitch, and it had been such a long time since she'd been able to make love to him. She'd missed his touch, his kiss. Of course, there'd been a stolen kiss here or there, but it only fueled a fire for which there seemed to be no extinguisher.

When Rachel and Londa got to the end of the pier where Mitch and James were waiting, they were surprised to see that the guys already had a taxi waiting for them.

James sat up front with the driver, and Londa sat in back with Mitch and Rachel. As Mitch placed his arm around Rachel's shoulder, she suddenly realized that there were no longer any boundaries between them. His cologne was intoxicating, and she thought it might just be her undoing.

They rode for about ten minutes to the first club, or more like a bar. They ran into a few people from the ship who told them about a bigger club across town where everyone else was. They all had enough drinks to get a good buzz going and jumped into another taxi to head to the other club. When they walked into the club, almost everyone from the ship was there. Mitch immediately dragged Rachel onto the floor. James and Londa were right behind. After about four dances, Rachel felt like her bladder was going to explode.

" Baby, I have to go to the bathroom. I'll be right back."
She told Mitch.

"All right but hurry up cause they jammin." He said.

Normally, Rachel would have asked Londa to go with her,
but she seemed to be having too much fun for Rachel to
disturb her, so she went alone.

When Rachel returned to the dance floor, Mitch was
dancing with Londa. Rachel noticed that James was
standing on the edge of the floor alone, so she asked him
to dance. James and Rachel walked out onto the dance
floor and began to dance right beside Mitch and Londa.
Rachel couldn't believe how much fun she was having. It
felt so good to get off the ship. She felt like she and Mitch
were finally having their first date.

After the song ended, both couples left the dance floor.
They were standing on the edge of the dance floor
watching everyone else have a good time. Londa and
James were all hugged up. Naturally, Rachel was feeling
affectionate as well, so she reached down to hold Mitch's
hand. She was completely shocked when he snatched his

hand away, and the look on his face nearly made her blood run cold.

"What's the matter with you?" Rachel asked, pain visible in her voice.

"Just get the hell away from me." Mitch snarled. " You ain't no better than the rest of them."

Rachel felt as if she'd been slapped in the face. " Mitch what did I do? Why are you acting like this?"

"You know what the hell you did; now you want to play all innocent." He said.

"What are you talking about? All I did was go to the bathroom. What you think I met somebody while I was in there?" She whined.

"You know what, I don't give a damn what you do; carry your ass! Screw whoever you want, and dance with whoever you want. I'm done with you!" He said as he walked away from her.

Finally, she understood, and the revelation hit her like a truck. He couldn't possibly think that she wanted James, but it was evident that he thought exactly that. Rachel didn't know whether to be flattered or insulted.

"Are you actually upset because I danced with James? Mitch, you were on the floor dancing with Londa when I came back from the bathroom. James was just standing there by himself, so we decided to join you guys. I don't see the problem in that. Londa wouldn't have a problem with that, and neither would James." She said.

"Like I said, I don't give a damn what you do, so carry your ass...Freak." He spat out the word "freak" like he'd just ate something bitter. He walked away from her again.

"Don't call me that!" Rachel said following close behind. In any other circumstance, she probably wouldn't have been so bold, but the two White Russians and three Rum and Cokes were taking their toll.

"Look, you need to get outta my face." Mitch said.

"So, you're not gonna talk to me?" Rachel asked. She was still trying so hard to keep her composure. Everyone from the ship was looking at them now, and Mitch seemed to love the attention.

"Look," he said raising his voice so that if there was a chance he didn't have the whole room's attention...he certainly did now. "It's over, Rachel; so just go on bout your business and I'll do the same. I told you. I don't care what you do." He seemed to have a satisfied smirk on his face now, knowing he'd thoroughly humiliated her.

Rachel just stared at him right in the eye. As much as she wanted to walk away from him and go cry the tears that were threatening to spill, she just could not let him treat her this way and not do or say anything. She had never been a fighter, but then again, she'd never been put in a situation where she had to fight, especially someone she loved. Now, she was standing there eye to eye, face to face, and toe to toe, and she was not gonna back down without a fight...for her dignity if nothing else!

All of a sudden Mitch started laughing at her. It was as if she was standing in front of him literally with egg on her face. "What the hell was so damn funny?" She thought. She could feel her face turning blood red. What happened after that was like a movie, and she was standing on the sidelines observing. Before Rachel knew it, she pushed Mitch. With all her might and with both hands at his chest, she pushed him so hard he almost fell. She wanted to laugh at the surprised look on his face, but she didn't dare. Still, he wasn't laughing anymore either.

"Bitch, what the hell's wrong with you?" He yelled.

Rachel had started the ball rolling, and she wasn't willing to back down now. "Why stop now?" She thought; she couldn't get any more embarrassed than she already was...so, full speed ahead!

She pushed him again. "Now, people were laughing at him," she thought. But in reality, they were laughing at them both. He started laughing at her again. The more he laughed, the madder she got. Rachel started to say things to purposely provoke Mitch.

"You ain't nothing but a punk. Why don't you hit me back? You're worse than a girl...I'm surprised you don't bleed once a month!" She spat. Rachel realized she'd pushed Mitch around the whole club with him laughing at her and calling her names, names that made her wonder what she ever saw in him. This couldn't be the same guy who actually asked if he could kiss her and not just assume that it was okay. She pushed him once more. She was out of control now. She pushed him so hard that he fell over a table. The club erupted in laughter. Rachel just stood over him, almost triumphantly.

She didn't run as he got to his feet, although she wanted to run. When Mitch got up, his back was to her. Suddenly, he swung around and back slapped her so hard she thought her head was going to explode. Before another blow could be landed, about five guys grabbed Mitch, and at least five girls grabbed Rachel. However, it was far from over. Mitch somehow got away from them, grabbed Rachel, and slapped her again. The girls let Rachel go, and she began to fight for what she felt like was her very life. The guys grabbed Mitch again, and this time started pulling him over toward the men's bathroom. The girls grabbed Rachel again, but not before she took her foot and tried to bury it in his behind. Finally, the girls got Rachel into the bathroom.

"Rachel, what happened?" Londa asked. "We all were havin' such a good time. Why did ya'll start fighting?"

"Remember when we first got here, and we were all dancing?" she asked.

"Yeah, that's what I mean. We was all having fun." She said.

"Well, when I came back from the bathroom and you and Mitch were dancing, I asked James to dance, and we came out there right next to ya'll." Rachel explained, crying now. The dam finally burst.

"Yeah, I remember." Londa said still wondering where the night went wrong.

"Well, he was mad because I danced with James!" Rachel cried. He started calling me all kinds of names. He said I was just like the rest of the Freaks on the Sound. I still don't know what I did wrong. Rachel was crying so hard now; Londa thought she was going to hyperventilate.

"You have got to be kiddin me. I know darn well Mitch ain't actin crazy over something so stupid." Londa said. She knew Mitch was very jealous about Rachel, but she never thought he would have a problem with Rachel dancing with James...Hell, he'd been was dancing with her at the time!

Just then, the door to the bathroom opened and Hannah came in. She went to Rachel, hugged her, and asked if she was all right.

"Yeah, I'll be okay." Rachel answered.

"Well, the guys put Mitch in a cab and sent him back to the ship. Rachel, when you're cleaned up, I'm gonna call you a cab to take you back to the ship." Hannah said. "Okay?"

"Okay." Rachel said, her head still spinning from the events of the night. Rachel washed her face and made sure her clothes were back where they were supposed to be. She walked outside with Hannah and Londa by her side. They waited with her til the cab came, deposited her inside, and went back inside the club. Rachel felt so alone. As much as she wanted to hate Mitch, she loved him so much that it felt like her heart would stop beating from the pain. When the cab pulled up to the pier, she got out, paid the driver, and started her long walk to the ship. Her mind wouldn't stop racing. She thought she and Mitch were so happy. She never thought it would end like this. Furthermore...she never thought in a million lifetimes that Mitch would ever lay a hand on her. Fresh tears rolled down her face as she walked up the bow. She quickly wiped them away. Rachel showed her I.D., requested permission to board, and once granted permission, walked on to her berthing.

Just as Rachel was passing Mitch's berthing, he swung open the door and came outside. She figured that he must have been waiting for her and heard her heels clicking on the deck. He looked at her with pure hatred in his eyes.

"You see what you did to my face?" He said angrily. He pointed at a very long scratch that started from almost in his left eye completely down his left cheek. The white meat was showing. Before Rachel could even utter an apology, he reached almost behind himself and returned with a back slap to the right side of her face. The blow spun Rachel all the way around, and she fell against the wall behind her and slowly slid to the floor. As she gathered herself and stood back up, Mitch simply turned around and walked back into his berthing like this was something he did every day. Rachel walked down the ladder to her own berthing with her hand to her cheek, crying silently. The last thing she wanted to do was wake anyone because then questions would be asked, and she would have to answer them. She got undressed, crawled into her rack, and cried herself to sleep.

CHAPTER TWENTY-ONE

Rachel felt a tugging, not physical, but she was being pulled just the same. Someone was calling her name, trying to bring her out of the oblivion, but she wanted to stay right where she was. It was quiet there...peaceful. It was getting louder now, and she could no longer ignore it. Finally, she felt herself being shaken.

"Rachel...Rachel, wake up. You okay?" Hannah was shaking her friend. She had a worried look on her face.

Rachel slowly opened her eyes. She tried to focus, but everything was still a bit blurry. Finally, Hannah's face came into clear view.

"Hey, it's almost one in the afternoon; you never sleep this late." Hannah said noticing a slight bruise on Rachel's right cheek. "You all right?" She asked concerned.

Rachel raised up on her elbows. "Well, that depends." She replied. "I dreamed that I showed my complete behind last night. Now, if it truly was a dream, then I am just peaches and cream. But, judging from the cannons going off in my head, and my face feeling like I used it to stop a truck, I have to believe that it all really happened."

"Yeah, it really happened." Hannah said smiling.

"Well, I couldn't have won the fight, according to the flashes of memory that was beginning to form in my pounding head...So what in the world could you be smiling at?" She said as she climbed out of her rack, wincing in pain.

"Girl, you was funny as hell!" Hannah exclaimed. "I still can't believe you and your little self was pushing Ghram like that. But girl, he is upset about his face. You should see the scar."

"I saw it." Rachel said. "I got a quick glance at it last night...just before he backhanded me through the wall." She said holding back tears. She felt badly that she'd hurt Mitch, and she wondered if he felt badly at all about what had happened between them last night. She also wondered if they would ever be the same, but she didn't see how they ever could go back to the way they were.

"I knew that bruise wasn't there when you left last night." Hannah said. "What happened?"

"He was waiting for me. He heard me walkin' by his berthing, and he came out the door just as I passed by. He was goin' off about his face. I tried to tell him I was sorry and that I didn't scratch him on purpose. It was the ring I had on." Rachel explained. "But he didn't want to hear nothing I said. Hannah, he looked at me like he hated me; then, he hit me so hard I fell into the wall of the Master at Arms shack. I thought I was gonna pass out it hurt so bad." She said. "By the time I got myself together enough to stand up, he'd already walked back into his berthing and closed the door." Rachel was crying again, and Hannah just reached out and held her.

FULL CIRCLE
Coming About
(The Sequel)

CHAPTER ONE

It had been a full 24 hours since Hannah had come to Rachel's rack and woke her up to Reality. Rachel had called Mitch every hour only to be told that he wasn't around. The ship was huge, but it wasn't so big that she and Mitch shouldn't have crossed paths by now. She looked on the Mess Deck, the Ship's store, and the Crew's Lounge. He was making sure that he didn't run into her.

Rachel felt like her heart had been broken just knowing that she'd hurt him. She'd sooner cut off her right hand than hurt him, or anyone. If he'd just stop avoiding her and answer one of her calls, she could explain that the scratch was an accident caused by the ring she'd been wearing.

"Well," She thought. "He has duty today, so he can't leave the ship." "He has to eat, so maybe I'll catch him on the Mess Deck. "If not, I'll see him at work tomorrow; He can't get out of that."

Hannah and Londa had told Rachel that the night before, when Rachel had duty, that Mitch had been at the club with some white girl from London. He'd been kissing all over her like he'd known her for years, and he'd just met her. It hurt terribly to know that she'd meant so little to him, that he could replace her so easily.

Rachel had decided that she didn't want to run into Mitch after all. She went up on the fantail and just watched the wake of the ship. The ocean was so beautiful to her. She loved the color of it, and especially the mysteriousness of it.

Londa had tried to get Rachel to go out with her and James, but Rachel wasn't in a partying mood. But she did promise she'd go the next night.

"What's up Miss Tiegs?" A familiar voice brought out of her thoughts. She turned to see Frank coming toward her. There were a few people out on the fantail with them, all in their own worlds.

"Hey, Frank." Rachel knew Frank had always been attracted to her, but for some unknown reason, she wasn't able to return his feelings. It wasn't because he wasn't fine, because he certainly was. But Mitch happened first, and the two were friends, so that was that.

"You Okay Rach?" He asked genuinely concerned. Just the fact that someone cared made tears well in Rachel's eyes.

"Yeah, I'm okay." She lied. She turned back to the ocean so that Frank wouldn't see the tears threatening to fall. But it was too late.

"No, you ain't." Frank insisted. "What the hell happened between you and Mitch?" He asked.

"I honestly don't know Frank." She answered. "One minute we were dancing, and the next minute he was calling me names and we were fighting!" Just recalling that night brought fresh tears. Rachel wiped them away.

"I'm sorry Rach," Frank said, now regretting asking. He hated to see Rachel in such pain, but he knew it was inevitable. Mitch never really cared about anyone but himself. But even Frank had to admit he'd never seen Mitch stay with a girl as long as he'd been with Rachel.

Frank had also never seen Mitch so jealous of any other female. He didn't' quite know what to make of it. Frank wanted to hold Rachel and comfort her, even protect her. But they were in uniform, and it wasn't allowed.

"I didn't mean to upset you, Rach," Frank said.

"It's okay Frank, really." Rachel said. "I'm just trying to wrap my mind around all that's happened." Rachel actually wished she could magically turn her love for Mitch off, or at least redirect it to someone like Frank. But, the heart wants what the heart wants, and there was nothing she could do but deal with her mess.

"I hear he has a new London girlfriend already." She joked halfheartedly. "Glad to know he's not losing any sleep over me." She added.

"Man he just tryin to play like he's not hurting." Frank said. "You know us men can't come off like we whipped or weak." He admitted smiling shyly. "Trust me; he don't give a damn about that girl. He just wanted to hurt you, and he knew somebody would come back and tell you." Frank said.

"Well," Rachel admitted sadly. "He accomplished what he set out to do. I couldn't be more hurt." She said.

"It's gonna be alright Rach," Frank said, now mad at Mitch and hating himself for making her sad. "You just stay strong and don't play the same game. Promise?" He said looking deep into her eyes.

"I promise Frank." Rachel said. "That not my style, I was raised better than that. All of a sudden, she burst out laughing like she'd just told the funniest joke.

Frank laughed too, not knowing what he was laughing at. "What the hell is so damn funny?" He asked.

"I just realized what I said...I was raised better than that. I was raised better than to get into a bar brawl too, but so much for that!" They both laughed hard.

"Thanks Frank, for making me laugh, and caring enough to check on me." She said. "It really means more than you know."

"Rachel, you know you always gonna be my girl." He said. "Come on, let's go inside, it's getting cold out here." He said jamming his hands into his pockets like he was freezing.

"You such a punk! It is not cold out here!" She teased.

"That's cause you from cold ass Jersey!" Frank said. "You don't know no better!"

"Whatever, you big baby." She laughed. "Come on, I don't' want you freezing because of me." She laughed.

They walked back down the portside and into the skin of the ship. When they got to the Mess Deck, Frank told Rachel goodbye. They shared a last smile, and she continued on to her berthing.

Rachel crawled into her rack, put on her headphones and just cried all over again. She prayed that the next day would be better. She was actually looking forward to going out with Londa. She felt like it could only get better from here.

ABOUT THE AUTHOR

Author Robbin Washington is a mom and wife. She also served in the United States military. This is her first novel.

Black Butterfly Books

is an imprint of

The Butterfly Typeface Publishing.

Contact us for all your
publishing & writing needs!

Iris M Williams
PO Box 56193
Little Rock AR 72215

www.butterflytypeface.com

www.ingramcontent.com/pod-product-compliance
Lightning Source LLC
Chambersburg PA
CBHW071138260626
47162CB00003B/832

* 9 7 8 1 9 4 7 6 5 6 5 4 3 *